HIDDEN BLADE

Soul Eater #1

PIPPA DACOSTA

'Hidden Blade'

#1 Soul Eater

Pippa DaCosta

Urban Fantasy & Science Fiction Author

Subscribe to her mailing list & get free ebooks.

Version 1.2

www.pippadacosta.com

Print ISBN-13: 978-1535097628

Print ISBN-10: 1535097620

SUMMARY

"They call me devil, liar, thief. In whispers, they call me Soul Eater. They're right. I'm all those things —and more."

Kicked out of the underworld and cursed to walk this earth for all eternity, Ace Dante finds solace in helping others avoid the wrath of the gods.

But when warrior-bitch, Queen of Cats, and Ace's ex-wife, Bastet, hires him to stop whoever is slaughtering her blessed women, Ace is caught between two of the most powerful deities to have ever existed: Isis and Osiris.

The once-revered gods aren't dead.

They're back.

And Ace is in their way.

Welcome to a New York where the ancient gods roam.

CHAPTER 1

Gods. *They're a pain in my ass,* I thought as my cell phone chirped in my pocket, alerting the four college kids inside the apartment that I was crouched on their balcony, watching them summon gods knew what from the underworld. It had to be a god calling me—too many millennia had given them the worst sense of timing.

The kids spotted me through the glass and bolted, falling over their array of ritual paraphernalia. If they scattered out of the apartment, it'd make scaring the shit out of them a whole lot harder.

I kicked the balcony door in, whipped my sawed-off shotgun free of its holster, and fired at their exit, peppering the door with lead. The kids yanked up short and whirled.

"Oh shit—oh shit—oh shit, we didn't know, man!" Hands up, they wailed in one long tirade. "We weren't doin' anythin'. Don't shoot us."

On and on their whining went, and on and on my cell tinkled, vibrating against my leg. Ignoring it all, I came to a stop at the edge of the elaborate summoning circle. A candle had toppled over, spilling wax across a papyrus scroll. The little flame licked at the scroll's upturned edge but didn't catch. Switching the shotgun to my left hand, I crouched, righted the candle, and flicked the papyrus around. I scanned the hieroglyphs scrawled from edge to edge. The penmanship was superb, more art than writing. Swirls and pen strokes danced beautifully, almost as though they were alive. Whoever had written this knew how to craft the ancient words in powerful and mostly forgotten ways. A sorcerer. A sinking sense of dread darkened my already somber mood.

"It's him," one of the kids hissed. "I told you... I told you he was following us. You didn't fuckin' listen, Jase."

"Shut up. Just shut up!" Jase snarled back, and then to me, he sniveled, "We were just messin' around."

Puffing out a sigh, I pinched the papyrus by its edges. The spellwork it contained was authentic. Kids these days. They had no fear and no clue. The spell nipped at my fingertips, trying to escape its bonds. I dangled it over the naked candle flame. A ripple of fire raced up the paper; fire liked volatile spells, especially those sanctioned by the underworld.

"He's gonna kill us," Jase whispered.

I snapped my gaze up. I could do worse than kill them. It had been a while since I'd indulged, but I could make an exception for spoiled, rich kids with too much time on their hands, especially since that one—Jase—and I already had a chat some weeks ago when I'd found him buying canopic jars.

He gulped loudly and made a brave attempt at staring back at me before dropping his eyes. Few could look me in the eye for long.

Finally, my cell stopped its incessant ringing and the quiet settled. Too quiet. New York didn't do quiet. I should have been hearing the endless whine of sirens or the bark of car horns. *I'm too late.*

I straightened. "What happened to kids screwing around

with Ouija boards? This here"—I flicked a hand at the well-crafted summoning circle—"this will get you killed."

"It's just some ancient Egyptian stuff."

My lips twitched dangerously close to a smile. Holstering the shotgun inside my coat, I reached behind my shoulder and curled my fingers around Alysdair's grip. The sword slid free from its leather scabbard with a satisfying gasp. There was something to be said for a two-handed sword, particularly the kind etched with spellwork exactly like that found on the scroll I'd just burned. Alysdair sang with magic. These kids wouldn't hear or feel it, but it wasn't meant for them. Strictly speaking, it wasn't meant for this world either—a little like me.

"Shit, man! You can't fuckin' do this!" They all started up again, bleating like penned sheep, all but one. The quiet one hadn't said a word since I'd kicked in the door and was doing a fantastic job of trying real hard to keep me from noticing him.

"C'mon, you're the Nameless One, right? The coat, the sword?" Jase spluttered, hope gushing through his words. "You're s'posed to be good."

I wasn't sure what surprised me more: the fact he'd heard of the Nameless One, or that these dumbass kids thought I was good.

"The Nameless One is an urban legend."

Pointing the sword tip at the floor, I scanned the apartment. The door was ten paces away; the balcony was closer. Two possible exits and I was in the middle, positioned exactly where I wanted to be.

"Besides," I drawled, "if he was real, you really wouldn't want him saving you."

Any hope of saving these kids had fled long before I arrived. The spellwork, the papyrus—heavy magic came at a high price. My job now was to contain the fallout.

My cell buzzed. "Poison" by Alice Cooper started playing from my pocket.

Quiet Guy kicked the glass coffee table, sending jagged pieces of glass raining over me. I flung up an arm too late to stop the shards from biting into my cheek. It only took a second, but the distraction lasted long enough for the summoned demon residing in Quiet Guy to snatch up a blade of glass and plunge it into his pal's neck. Things got messy real fast after that.

A hail of screams erupted. Blood sprayed in a wide arc as the kid dropped. The demon inside Quiet Guy let out a triumphant howl, and the two remaining kids did the only sensible thing: they bolted out the door.

I lunged at the demon, Alysdair aglow, but being free, probably for the first time in its long life, the demon wasn't about to let the sight of Alysdair frighten it. Scuttling back—its movements broken and twitchy inside its human host—the demon clawed its way up the wall and onto the ceiling. Its human mouth split impossibly wide, and a long, whip-like black tongue lashed out.

It expected me to fall back. Those tongues were barbed. Any sane person would have run out the door with the kids, but I snatched the tongue out of the air, flicked it around my wrist, and yanked. I wasn't *any* sane person. Technically, I wasn't a person.

The demon heaved back, jerking me forward.

Wrestling with a demon's tongue wasn't how I'd expected this evening to go.

"Give up now—" I started, but the tongue knotted back on itself, reeling me closer. "And I'll let you live."

My boots slipped. Tighter and tighter the tongue coiled up my forearm, bicep, and shoulder, until the demon had me dangling, my boot toes scuffing the floor.

The demon chuckled, the sound of it like metal grinding

against metal—an abhorrent, not-of-this-world sound that set my teeth on edge.

"Lost your bite... Namelessssss One..." it hissed around its tongue, outside my mind as well as burrowing the words deep inside my thoughts.

"I know a girl like you." I tightened my dangling grip on Alysdair. "All tongue."

The demon had begun distorting its victim's body. The face was swollen and flushed purple, as though Quiet Guy had been run through a trash compactor. The eyes, so fragile, had been one of the first things to go. They had turned to mush and were dribbling from their sockets. Crimson flames danced inside the dark, hollow sockets, seemingly deeper than a human skull could account for, as if reaching right into the soul. The eyes really were the windows to the soul, and Quiet Guy's was no longer home. Soon, there would be little left of the kid. Once that happened, the demon would become virtually unstoppable and the no-bullshit New Yorkers would have more to worry about than the alligators in the sewers, like the type of problem that ate small children and used their bones to pave the way for more of its ilk.

"Don't get me wrong," I pushed the words through my teeth, "there's a lot the right girl can do with her tongue, but my friend's is as sharp as a dagger and cuts like one too."

"Join me... Soul Eater...you were powerful once...could be again..."

I pretended to think about it while locking eyes with those glowing red coals. The deeper I looked, the deeper the creature's needs and desires clawed into my mind. There was no light in this one, only poisonous, devouring darkness.

"I don't do demon."

I heaved the sword around and thrust it upright, sinking it deep into the demon's gut. The demon screamed the way only otherworldly creatures could, as though the sword had cleaved its soul in two. I drove Alysdair right up to its damn hilt. A familiar spell pushed from my lips, which would have been the perfect end to this little dance had the demon's tongue not unraveled and dropped me like a stone. I fell, dragging Alysdair down with me, and landed in a crouch.

The demon scuttled along the ceiling, down the wall, and out the door, leaving a trail of bubbling blood behind it.

I spat a curse and dashed after it, my ringtone still belting out Alice Cooper and how his girl's lips were venomous poison.

CHAPTER 2

Body number two lay sprawled in the stairwell, neck broken. I stepped over the corpse and jogged up the stairs, following the splatters of blood toward the roof. The demon would eventually kill the third kid too; they always killed their summoners—the people who potentially had power over them.

Shoving through a door, the stairwell spat me out into a biting winter wind. Snow swirled and patted against my face, softening the sounds of New York's usual din of traffic.

Alysdair in hand, hieroglyphs glowing pale green along her blade, I stepped into a few inches of snow cover and bounced my gaze around the rooftop's clutter. Storage boxes, an elevator motor enclosure, some other jagged shapes silhouetted against the glistening skyline, but no obvious demons. Beyond the roof, a high-rise loomed, its windows aglow. With the gunshot and the bodies, someone would call the cops and soon. I had to get this done fast, before the demon sprouted wings.

"I've reconsidered," I called out, following the trail of

blood. My boots crunched in the snow, so there was no use in trying to move quietly. "You and me, I can make that work."

The grinding laughter returned, but the wind gathered it up and tossed it around the rooftop. "You are weak..."

"Says the demon with a hole in its gut," I muttered. "You're going to die here, you must know that."

The demon could shift its shape and escape. Given enough time, it could hole up somewhere and lick its wounds. I couldn't let that happen. A demon loose in a city like New York would be a public relations nightmare. Naturally, it would be my fault. Most screwups were, if you asked the gods.

"You are not free to make a deal, Nameless One."

"How's that?" I inched up against the elevator enclosure and eyed the trail of blood leading out of sight around the corner.

"Your soul is owned by another." The words tumbled through the air, but their source was close. "I tasted *him* on you."

I winced. That truth cut too close to the bone for comfort. If word got out I was Ozzy's bitch, nobody would hire me. Shit, nobody would come within ten feet of me. If the demon didn't have to die before, it did now.

Enough talk. Talking with demons—and listening to them —was a surefire way of getting your mind devoured. This one had spent long enough probing my thoughts to pick up on my fears. They were good at that—planting seeds that would later grow into toxic doubts until you fancied yourself a long walk off a short balcony. I hadn't dealt with a demon of this caliber in a while; clearly, I was rusty.

"Slippery things, souls." I lifted Alysdair and wrapped both hands around her handle, letting the sword pull on my magical reserves. "They're surprisingly easy to lose and damned difficult to get back."

I lunged around the corner and got a face full of contorted demon chest. Alysdair plunged through cleanly, slicing deeper than the metal alone would have allowed for, and sank into that fetid thing inside—its soul. A flicker snagged at my resolve—a twitch from my past, of how good it would be to drink its soul down. It *had* been a long time, but this was Alysdair's moment to shine, not mine. A soul that black, I didn't need the weight.

The demon let out its ear-piercing screech. Its claws raked at my sword arm to cut off the source of its agony, but its red-eyed glow was fading as Alysdair fed. The sword sang in my grip until the deed was done, and the demon collapsed into a pile of loose skin and putrid flesh.

The after buzz tapped at the part of my mind that went to deeper, darker things every time Alysdair got her kick and I didn't—the *what-ifs* and *just-a-little-bits*. With a growl, I staggered back, grateful the snow was swirling faster now and covering up the grisly evidence.

"Poison" blared again from my pocket.

"For Sekhmet's sake!" I wiped Alysdair clean on my duster coat and drove her home inside her sheathe, snug between my shoulder blades. Then I snatched the cell from my pocket. "Shu, by the gods, this had better be good or I will come back there and shove your little statue of Ra up your—"

"Ace."

Gods be damned, I'd worked with Shukra long enough to recognize that arctic tone in her voice. "That's my name, peaches. Don't wear it out."

Sirens wailed nearby—too nearby. I strode to the edge of the roof and didn't need to look far to see the blue and white lights bathing the walls of the opposite building. It was too late to clean up the mess.

"There's a goddess in your office. I suggest you don't make her wait."

The line went dead.

A goddess in my office? That didn't narrow it down. There were more goddesses topside than you could shake a crook and flail at. Time to make a quick exit and leave the cops with more questions than they had any hope of answering. I tucked my cell away. I broke into a jog, the rooftop's edge approaching fast. I picked up speed, wondered too late if the gap between the buildings might be wider than I'd guesstimated, and leaped into the dark.

⊙⁂⊙

IGNORING GODS DIDN'T MAKE THEM GO AWAY. I'D TRIED. But that didn't mean I couldn't eek out some pleasure by making the bitch wait. I *was* on my way to my office, but I just happened to drop by Toni's bar and order a few shots first. Antonio was more than eager to oblige, and I figured I owed it to Toni to prop the bar up like I did most nights after a job, especially when the job flirted with the kind of illicit desires that had gotten me thrown out of the underworld— or *Duat,* to give the place it's proper name.

Toni drifted over, saluting me with the bottle of whatever he'd been serving me—something syrupy and potent. I placed my hand over the glass and shook my head. The idea was to arrive late, not drunk, although the thought of seeing the look on Shu's face did appeal to me. She wasn't immune to angry gods quite like I was. A minor god had once gotten the wrong idea about Shu and me and figured he could get to me by hurting her. I didn't answer the ransom, and as soon as Shu got free, she ripped his insides out via his throat. Happy days.

"Ace, right?" a sweet voice asked, wrenching me out of my thoughts. "Hi, I'm Rosie. I work right across the street."

I looked at her and then at Antonio, who shrugged and left to tend to the rest of his flock, and finally at the door like

I might be able to see the place she'd mentioned through it. "The accountants?"

"Yeah." She beamed, tucked her short blond hair behind her ear and leaned against the bar. "I...er... I've seen you around a few times, and..."

She was talking, and I probably should have been listening, but my mind was still going over that tick, that little hook that had dug itself in right when the demon had died, that little voice that said the demon's soul should have been mine. That voice was almost as old as I was. I thought I'd kicked it to the curb long ago.

Rosie's smooth hand touched my arm, startling me back into the bar. She smiled like she was waiting for me to say something. I had no idea what. She was looking for company, but if she knew what I was she'd run, screaming.

I tossed a few dollars on the bar and slipped off my stool. "I gotta get to work."

Sinking my hands into my jacket pockets, my fingers brushed a familiar gold band. I slipped the ring over my ring finger, pushed through the door, and ducked my head against the flurries of snow.

I'd made the goddess wait long enough.

CHAPTER 3

Opening the door to the rented office space Shukra and I shared, I almost kicked a streak of black fur as it darted around my ankles and disappeared down the stairwell.

"Shu! Keep the damn door closed!" I slammed the door to drive my point home. "I hate cats."

A headache was trying to hammer its way out of my skull through my eyeballs, my cheek was throbbing—probably from the tiny bits of glass I couldn't pick out—and I was still sore over the new claw marks in my coat. The cherry on top of my fantastic night would be the goddess waiting behind my closed office door.

"Ace," Shu said as she strode down the hall, hips swaying hypnotically like a cobra in a pantsuit.

I'd once condemned her to Hell. Her soul was the blackest I'd ever seen. She should have been devoured, and yet here she was, a blight on my life, striding toward me like she owned the goddamn place. *Half* owned it. My hatred for her burned as fiercely as it had on the day I'd weighed the light in her soul and found it lacking, and it was only matched by the vicious hatred she felt for me. We had that in common, at least.

"You're not gonna like it," she said, pulling up outside my office door. Her lips cut blood-red lines through her golden complexion. She still carried the darker skin tone of the east, even after all this time. She wore her oil-black hair up in a ponytail so tight it pulled her cheekbones up with it. I hadn't been lying about the woman with a tongue like a knife—or exaggerating. She had the kind of sultry good looks that lured men and women close so she could tear their hearts out and eat them while her victims died watching. Disgust and hatred had saved me that fate.

"When have I ever liked anything you've said?" I told her and reached for the office door.

"This one—"

"I've got this." I opened the door and my guts fell through the floor. My bravado, the thumping pain in my head, and the sickening sense that the world wasn't done screwing with me all came to a screeching halt. Never had a second dragged on for so long an eternity.

Goddess Bastet—Queen of Cats, Warrior Bitch, and my ex-wife—was sitting in my chair. She'd propped her boots, buckled up to the knee, on my desk and was plucking at her elaborately painted nails with my decorative letter opener. In her hands, that letter opener was a deadly weapon.

"Get out of my chair," I growled.

"Technically, the chair is half mine." She spoke slowly, leisurely, taking her time because she had immeasurable amounts of it.

"Take the chair and get out." I even stepped aside and held the door open for her like a gentleman.

Shu stood down the hallway, glaring daggers. "She's a client."

My headache was back and thumping down my neck. I should have stayed at Antonio's.

"Conflict of interest," I blurted, scrambling for any excuse to be done with this day, my ex-wife, and Shu's eternally pissed-off expression.

"You were always interested in conflict before." This came from the smooth lips of my ex-wife. She could sit there as calm and relaxed as she liked, but like any cat, she could go from tame to rabid if I glanced at her the wrong way.

Closing my eyes, I pinched the bridge of my nose and counted to three—that was as far as I got before my chair creaked, drawing my eye back to Bast as she rose gracefully to her feet. She was tall and lean and had a powerful gait, like the top cat cruising her territory. That's what had first caught my eye; after a few hundred years, I'd been looking for a challenge and found it in her.

She wore some kind of belted waistcoat with an array of buckles and long fingerless gloves that ended at the elbow. Short black hair clung close to her cheeks, giving her a wild, foreboding flair, as though she'd sooner stab you as say hello. And yet her mouth was smooth, her lips soft, and her words like silk, and her touch...

I told myself I was looking for weapons when I roamed my gaze up her thighs and over her hips. I knew every inch of her and how she used it all.

"Shu," I cleared my throat, "give us a minute."

Shu was already halfway down the hall when she called back, "Anything gets broken, it comes out of your paycheck."

I closed the door and pressed my back against it. Bast had taken up a spot leaning against my desk. She'd set the letter opener down beside her, still within reach. I didn't actually think she'd go to all the trouble of hiring me only to stab me, but jilted women did crazy things. Jilted goddesses were damn right psychotic.

She blinked bottle-green, cat-like eyes and clasped her hands loosely in front of her.

"Do I talk first," I asked, "or should we wait for the tension to kill me?"

"Someone is killing my blessed. I want you to find out who."

"Someone is killing cats?"

"No." Her eyes narrowed. "Were you even paying attention when we were married?"

All gods had obsessions, little quirks to get them through millennia of endless boredom. Her *thing* was cats. I'd once woken in her bed surrounded by hundreds of felines—or maybe it had been thirty. Thirty cats sure felt like a hundred when they were watching you sleep. She *was* a cat—a big-ass jungle cat with claws like *janbiya* daggers who liked to pretend she was a person, or maybe it was the other way around. The lines had blurred. A lot had blurred in twenty years. I couldn't be expected to remember everything a goddess chose to bless.

What the hell else could be blessed by Bastet? Warriors, swords, ninjas? "I have no idea."

"Pregnant women."

"Right. That. Of course. Pregnant women."

Her mouth curled at one side, tucking into her cheek. "You haven't changed."

I *had*, just not recently. "Shu will look into it."

"No."

"Bast."

She lifted her head at my tone and fixed those penetrating green eyes on mine. I hesitated, my argument stalling. If I spent too long looking into her eyes, I'd see into her soul. I'd been down that road before. I no more wanted to see the truth than she wanted me to see it. Breaking the visual connection before the magic could take hold, I sauntered around my desk and dropped into my chair.

"My schedule is packed. I really don't have the time."

"I saw. You must be keeping Antonio busy."

She had been rooting through my desk. I made a mental note to yell at Shu later, not that she could have stopped a goddess from helping herself to my office, but I could still lay into my business partner. It would make me feel better.

"Bast, you and me...we've been there." I rummaged around my top drawer, trying to look busy. She might get the point and leave. "Let's not get tangled up again. Shu is better suited to—"

"Shukra is a condemned soul tied to you because Osiris has a twisted sense of humor." Bast planted her hands on my desktop and leaned in, driving her glare down on me. "I will not entrust the lives of my blessed to a foul being who should have been devoured centuries ago."

I couldn't argue with her words, or with the venom in them, but working with Bast on something like this? I already knew where it was headed. We'd end up fighting, which was never a pretty sight, the guilt would pile on, and there might even be some sex in there somewhere—angry sex, the toxic kind.

"You're wearing our wedding band?"

I looked at my hand, surprised to find the incriminating evidence right there on my finger. "I...er..."

Damn, she was scrutinizing me again with those cat eyes.

"You left me, remember?" Bast said.

I remembered precisely how her knee had found my balls.

"You want the ring back?" I gave the ring a twist, but it wasn't budging.

"No, I want your help." She straightened and seemed to grow three inches. When she spoke, her voice carried a compulsion—a decent one too and heavy enough to scratch at my mind. "Women in Queens are dying. Women blessed by me, in my territory. My chosen. This is personal, and I don't trust anyone else to do what needs to be done."

Trust. We'd trusted each other once. Funny how that worked. Gods didn't trust easily, and especially not other gods.

Her compulsion slid right off. She probably wasn't aware she'd cast it, seeing as trying to compel me to do anything was a waste of magic. The fact she had made that mistake told me how much this meant to her. She wouldn't have returned unless this was important. Her last words to me had been along the lines of, *"If I see you again in a thousand years, it'll be too soon."*

Twenty years was a blink to her. Maybe if I took the job and we stayed out of each other's way, I could get this done. Business was slow. The gods and their minions were unusually quiet. I needed the cash, needed this job, just not the baggage that came with it.

"You have to help, Ace." The softness in her voice did me in, and I was about to agree, when she added, "For our daughter."

"What?"

"I didn't tell you because—"

"Wait."

She waited. I opened my mouth, stalled, and closed my mouth.

"What?" I could hear my heart pounding right alongside the throbbing in my head. Daughter? "Back up a second."

"She's nineteen—and pregnant."

A crazy little laugh slipped free. No. No way. Not in a thousand years would I believe this shit. "Really? You're running with that cliché? I was going to say yes, but now... now...tell the sucker he has a kid and he'll do anything?" I grinned, the laughter working its way to the surface again. "No thanks."

"I'm not lying."

I clamped my jaw so hard my teeth ached. A daughter. It was a lie. It had to be.

"You know what? I'll let the lies slide. If what you're saying is true and women in Queens are dying, I'll look into it. Email me all the information you have." I was done with her and this conversation. I just wanted her out of my office so I could raid the vodka in my bottom drawer. "But don't lie to me, Bast. Okay? Not you. *Don't.*"

I weighted the last word with my own compulsion, enough so she'd feel it and know I wasn't screwing around.

She pulled a photo from her pocket and slammed it down on my desk like it was a smoking gun. "She has your eyes."

Then she stormed out, slamming the door behind her with all the dramatic flare that goddesses possessed.

Twisting off the cap of the vodka bottle, I didn't bother with a glass and gulped down a few generous mouthfuls. And then I wished I hadn't as it burned my throat and threatened to come back up again.

The picture was sitting near the far edge of my desk, within reach, if I wanted to believe. I glared at it, my heart trying to hammer itself into something colder and harder. After twenty years, she'd decided to come back into my life, sit in my chair, and tell me I had a daughter. There should have been a law against women like her. Goddesses didn't abide by laws, only those of their own making, and even then they were more like guidelines.

I launched out of my seat, reached across the desk, snatched up the picture, and dumped it in the trash. There, that was dealt with. No picture. No guilt.

Bast and me, we'd had fun, until the lies started—my lies. Until I'd made the mistake of reading her soul.

My door rattled and flung open.

"I'm not in the mood," I groaned.

Shukra leaned against the doorframe and examined her nails. She'd stay that way until I acknowledged her. Hours, if necessary, just to win.

"Fine. What?"

"You're popular today. Ozzy called."

"He called?" First Bast, now Osiris? "On a phone?"

"No, via a séance." She rolled her eyes. "He wants to see you."

The vodka in my gut churned. "Now?"

She hesitated, a wicked smile crawling onto her lips. "Tomorrow morning. Ten a.m. sharp, Acehole."

And with that, she left, but her tinkling laughter sailed all the way up the hallway.

I side-eyed the vodka bottle. "Just you an' me."

I scooped it up and lifted it to my lips.

CHAPTER 4

"**Y**ou look like my dog."

I squinted one eye at Nick "Cujo" Jones. He didn't have a dog.

"After it died," he added with a snort and then wheeled his wheelchair down his hall.

I followed, my head stuffed with cotton and my gut as fragile as a sacrificial virgin.

"I didn't think you folks got hangovers?" Cujo said from farther down the hall, inside his kitchen.

I wasn't hungover—hangovers were for lightweights. What I was feeling was more like halfway dead. Any further and I'd be back in the underworld.

"Takes some doing." My voice sounded as dry and broken as my insides.

Cujo's ground-floor apartment smelled of incense and marijuana. The incense was for deterring unwanted spirits, and the marijuana, that was for medicinal purposes—probably. I walked by dusty, decades-old framed photos of younger Cujo all buttoned up in his NYPD uniform, his cap tucked under his arm, and his smile fresh and bright. He'd been on the job for a few years before he had the misfortune of wandering into the crossfire between two bickering gods. He'd lived, but he would never walk again. After seeing enough of the impossible, he'd decided to start digging into the supernatural while he recovered, and a year later, he came to me, cash in his pocket and hungry for revenge. I'd declined, telling him he was better off forgetting it, but he hadn't forgotten. He'd tried to hire me countless times since, and somewhere along the line, I'd started asking him for favors. Fifteen years on, he had yet to cash in his favors, but he would.

"Must have been a rough job?" Cujo asked in that gruff, no-bullshit tone of his. He'd filled out since his recruit photos. His dark hair was peppered with gray, and the years had weathered his face, drawing deep lines around his eyes and mouth. Age ate at some people, whittling them away, but not Cujo. The years had honed him into a hard-ass.

"Demons and dead bodies I can deal with. It's the ex-wife who did me in."

"Ah." He whirled his chair next to the kitchen table and leaned back. "What you got for me?"

I handed over the picture Bast had left with me, the one I'd dumped in the trash and then fished out again before passing out at my desk. "Nineteen. Pregnant. Lives in Queens."

Cujo took the picture, ran his critical gaze over it, and scratched at his whiskered chin. When he looked up, he clearly had a question on his lips.

"Don't say it," I suggested.

He shrugged. "Uh-huh. It's probably the light."

"No, really. Don't."

He tilted the photo side-on. "Maybe it's the camera angle or a lens flare caught in her eyes, made them glow a little?"

To keep my mind busy and my thoughts off the girl's

uncanny likeness, I searched Cujo's cupboard, found a glass, and filled it from the faucet. All the while, Cujo's gaze rode my back like a devil on my shoulder.

"I need to know if she is nineteen and if she's showing any signs of—"

"Magic, hoodoo, spooky shit?" Cujo had a knack for reducing the terrifying into a joke. He took it all, the truth about the gods and their many beasts, in his stride.

"Just do some digging. See what you can find out about her."

"Right-oh," he said with too much enthusiasm.

I gulped down the water, waited to see if it would reappear anytime soon, and then turned to face Cujo's crafted expression of innocence. "Keep this quiet. If anyone discovers—"

"That you couldn't keep it in your pants?"

"Bastard." A grin broke out across my lips.

Cujo arched an eyebrow. "Are there any more little Aces running around out there you want me to look for while I'm at it?"

"Gods, I hope not. One is enough."

"Nobody ever teach you about protection in the underworld?"

I spluttered a laugh. Where I came from, traditional laws of nature did not apply. "It's more complicated than that."

He leaned back in his chair, wrestling his smile under control. "It's been a while, but I seem to remember the whole process was pretty straightforward."

"My ex-wife is a cat in her spare time. Insert Tab A into Slot B doesn't cut it when you're screwing gods."

He let loose his chuckle. "I should have known. Nothing is ever simple around you." He looked again at the picture. "Pretty. Must be her mother's influence."

"Ha, ha."

"What god did she annoy to get lumped with you as her dad?"

"Possible dad," I corrected and cringed. "What, you don't think I'm parent material?"

"Oh, sure." He crossed his arms over his chest, but that glint in his eye told me he wasn't done. "It's not like I'm constantly keeping your ugly mug off police records. Then there's the weird shit that follows you. Put it this way: I wouldn't want Chantal within five square miles of you."

There was no chance of that. Chantal, Cujo's teenage daughter, looked at me like she'd seen my soul, knew exactly what I was made of, and was distinctly unimpressed. Most people had attuned survival instincts that kept them out of my path. But Chantal wasn't most people, and confrontation was her middle name. The first time we'd met, she'd asked me if I used my looks to manipulate and warned me that if I tried any of that shit with her, she'd set Cujo on me. I couldn't blame her. As far as she knew, I was in my late twenties, early thirties and an inexplicable "family friend." The type of "friend" her father wouldn't talk about. She didn't trust my vagueness. Never had. Never would. At least her instincts were accurate there. Outside of the Egyptian pantheon, Chantal was right up there on my "avoid at all costs" list.

Cujo had a point. I wasn't father material. "I'm hoping the girl has nothing to do with me."

He shot me a look, something like, "Keep telling yourself that," and said, "I'll run the girl through the NYPD systems and let you know what I find. That's what got you wasted, huh?"

"That"—my insides twisted—"and Osiris's summons."

Cujo's smile died a slow death and his cheeks lost some of their ruddy color. It took a lot to pale Cujo. "Shit." He shook his head. "Man, it's been a few years since the last time?"

I nodded, not trusting my voice.

He ran a hand through his hair and sighed. "I wish I could do more for yah."

"I appreciate the thought."

There was nothing Cujo, or anyone, could do. When the god of the underworld whipped up a curse, he didn't leave loopholes or wiggle room. I'd spent a few hundred years searching for one. Now I just lived with it, like I had to live with Shukra's putrid soul bound to mine.

"There's some whiskey under the sink," Cujo offered. "If you want some Dutch courage."

"Thanks, but my insides won't survive. Might take you up on a drink once I'm done with him though."

Facing Osiris drunk would only make a bad situation worse. I wouldn't be able to keep my mouth shut and would probably end up with another curse strangling my already battered soul.

Cujo's smile turned sympathetic. "At least he can't kill you, right?"

Somehow, I smiled, and not for the first time, I secretly wished Osiris had.

CHAPTER 5

I parked my Ducati next to Ozzy's black Tesla, kicked the bike over on its stand, and fantasized about bringing Alysdair along for the ride. I didn't know if the sword could devour a god's soul, but I'd give it another shot. I'd tried before and failed spectacularly. It wasn't Osiris who'd taken umbrage at my assassination attempt. He'd found my efforts highly entertaining. Isis, on the other hand...

I shivered, swung my leg over the bike, palmed my keys, and gouged a deep line along the side of the Tesla, clipping every panel, and then I flicked my collar up and approached the mansion's entrance. After being around for as long as I had, I realized life was about taking the little pleasures as and when I could find them, because tomorrow, someone could rip them all away.

Gravel and snow crunched under my boots and the harsh New York wind bit at my bruised face as I stopped at the door. I pressed the bell and heard the chime echo inside. Any hope that Ozzy might have forgotten about his summons quickly died when his hired muscle opened the door. The guards frisked me, like always. I couldn't imagine anyone would be stupid enough to smuggle in a weapon (apart from me, that one time).

"Ozzy out back?" I asked Bob, the guard. Bob wasn't his real name, just the one I'd given him. Bob never smiled. I wouldn't have much to smile about if I were in Osiris's service either.

"You'll find the mayor waiting for you same place as always," Bob replied.

Believe it or not, there wasn't a whole load of difference between New York and what most people called Hell. Swap the people out for demons, the politicians for gods, throw in the cutthroat family drama, amp up the mood lighting, and turn the Hudson into a river of souls, and welcome to home sweet home. Osiris was mayor here and a god back home. If he had it his way, he'd be a god here too. He probably believed he already was.

Osiris's house was a museum, all dressed up for show. I'd never seen anyone out front, in the residence, and doubted Osiris and his wife did more than walk through the pretense of being average New Yorkers.

I sauntered through the cathedral-like foyer, down a red-carpeted hall, and into the study. I'd once admired the ancient books and array of Egyptian artifacts locked inside the glass cabinets, but now I barely spared them a glance. This wasn't a social call. If I made the god wait any longer, I'd start to feel the hold he had over me; that was probably part of the reason my hangover was hanging around like the mistress at a wake.

The theatrics of opening the secret bookcase door had long ago lost its novelty and only served to remind me of the egotistical showman I was about to drop to my knees for.

The sight greeting me at the foot of the hidden staircase was, unfortunately, a typical one: women and men in various states of undress. Robed servers tended to their every need while they gorged themselves on the banquet of food, wine, and sex. The warm, wet air smelled like jasmine, cinnamon, indulgence, and sweat.

Overdressed in my coat, I garnered a few long, lingering glances as I picked my way through the revelers, keeping my eyes front and center. I didn't want to know who they were—probably local officials and celebrities. Many of them likely had no choice but to be here. Osiris could be undeniably persuasive.

I took a wrong turn, easily done when every doorway was draped in gossamer curtains, and stumbled in on lurid sights I hadn't seen before and didn't wish to see again. By the time I found the right section, my heart was thudding fast and heavy and my breaths were coming on a little too hard.

Heat rolled out of the back chamber, the likes of which I hadn't known since the weighing chambers. I wiped my hands on my pants, gulped down what would probably be my last free breaths, and pushed through the drapes. It took a long, drawn out three seconds to read the mood in the room, three seconds in which my stride stuttered and instantly told two of the worlds' most powerful deities exactly what I didn't want them to know: that I'd prefer to be anywhere else but here with them.

Isis was lounging in an elaborate golden chair, jewels glittering in her raven-black hair. The fabric of her skintight dress was as thin and colorful as butterfly wings—for all the parts of her it covered up. Her golden skin shone, damp from exertion, as did her eyes, which were fixed across the room on her husband (and brother) seated at the end of a large bed. A woman was currently on her knees, worshipping his cock with her mouth.

The pair knew I was there, despite neither of them having acknowledged me. I gritted my teeth and waited, eyes fixed on the traditional relief of Osiris tucked inside an alcove along the back wall. I couldn't do much about the noise, except be grateful I hadn't eaten.

"Nameless One..." Osiris drawled. "Come here."

My heart turned to stone. The compulsion wrapped around my flesh and bones and buried inside the parts of me deeply rooted in this realm. Forward I went, one foot in front of the other, until I stood beside the god, unable to turn my gaze away from the woman's bobbing head and rhythmic hand. I could close my eyes—and did, briefly—but that only made it worse.

If he asked me to suck him, I'd bite it off.

I waited, willing the time forward so I could get back to my little office and my paranormal clients with their mundane enquires that paid the bills and kept my mind from straying. I even considered being nice to Shu—anything to get me out of this waking nightmare.

"This is taking too long," Isis said, the ice in her voice cutting.

"It's called sharing, Light of my Life. You had your—" Osiris's breath caught, and he held it. The girl's wet lips worked faster. The god leaned back, bracing his arms on the bed behind him, and breathed, "Right there."

I shut my eyes and tried to recall the last time I'd ordered stationary. The office had to be due for another batch of pens. I'd get one of those handmade, leather-bound planners too, with all the fancy address cards and pockets.

Osiris grunted, deep and low, and then let out a strangled groan that rolled on and on until I wished I had brought Alysdair along so I could fall on the sword and put an end to my misery.

"No, no..." Osiris crooned. "You don't swallow the nectar. Spit, dear."

She did. I heard everything—smelled it too. Bile burned the back of my throat.

It had been a year, maybe two, since Osiris had summoned me. In that time, I'd deliberately forgotten how much I despised him. There was a time I'd screamed at him, raged, thrown my fists, and gotten myself strung up for my efforts. Now I endured.

I opened my eyes to see Isis sashaying toward us. Nature didn't make women like her. Infinite power rippled through the air she carved through. She wore her beauty like armor and walked like time and decay couldn't touch her. Slim and lithe, she didn't look as though she had the strength to topple empires, but she could and she had—many times.

She planted something smooth, thin, and cool in my hand. I blinked down, recognized it as a dagger, and wondered if I could plunge it between Osiris's ribs before either of them could stop me.

"Don't move." The compulsion ran steel rods through my spine, locking me down.

The god stood, naked but for a plain cotton robe. He had a supremely proud face, a strong jaw, and fierce, long-lashed dark eyes. Without a word, he inspired the best in men— honor and loyalty—and a ferocious adoration from women, the type that could turn a mother against her child.

I had a blade in my hand and stood a few inches from his sun-baked chest, and he knew I wanted nothing more than to ram the blade into his heart and twist it in deep.

He appraised my scruffy coat and damp hair. His eyes moved to my face, where he probably hoped to find ammunition to use against me, but I'd learned long ago to keep my intentions far from my expression. He saw only boredom, compliance, and obedience. A snarl pulled at my lip. I swallowed, holding the rage deep inside.

He yanked the girl to her feet. Her pink tongue darted out, licking at a dribble of semen.

"Kill her," Osiris said.

Panic wrapped around my heart. I fought to pull back my body, to somehow get a grip on its flesh, but all I could do was watch from inside my own skin as I lifted the dagger. *No, no!*

Osiris's warm hand curled around my neck. "Stop."

Relief lifted the terror. Through it all, I'd struggled to keep my face an expressionless mask.

He jerked me forward, so close that his finely kohl-lined eyes were all I could see. "I'm just screwing with you."

Gold rimmed his wide, black pupils and bled through the darker hazel color in his irises. He held me under his command, trapping me in my body, and burrowed his gaze deep into mine, knowing the longer he and I locked stares, the likelier it was I'd see into his soul. I closed my eyes, cutting off the magic before it could take root. His soul was not something I had any wish to witness.

Osiris shoved me back, rocking me onto my back foot, and took the dagger from my hand. "Sit, have a drink, relax."

I would do all those things because I didn't have a choice. Stumbling to the table, I fell into a chair and poured myself wine from a crystal jug. I despised how my hand shook, sloshing wine over the tabletop. I would get through this, just like I had every other time.

"How's business?" the god asked, draping himself into the chair next to mine, sprawling like a lion in the sun. He set the dagger down between us. So close, so tempting.

"Could be better." I tasted the wine, found it sweet and sickly, but swallowed it anyway. It slipped all the way down and churned in my empty gut. "Could be worse."

Isis and the girl—whoever she was—were getting intimate in my peripheral vision. This was par for the course when it came to Osiris. As well as holding the title of God of the Underworld, he also happened to be the God of Fertility, and he was liberal with his blessings.

He poured himself some wine and cradled the glass stem between his long fingers while leaning back in his chair and looking me over. A smile teased the edges of his mouth. He was probably thinking of all the ways he could pull my strings.

"I don't hear much about you. Just the occasional whisper here and there..."

"We—Shu and I—we prefer it that way. Our clients appreciate discretion." And most of them didn't want news of their mistakes getting back to Osiris.

"Ah, Shukra... How is she?"

Still tied to my soul, you twisted fuck.

"Fine." I swallowed more wine, my throat constricting. I couldn't stop drinking, not until he released the compulsion. If I vomited it back up, he'd only make me drink more. I willed the wine to stay down. "Why did you summon me?"

Osiris drew in a deep breath through his nose. He crossed his legs and sent his gaze around the room. "News from the underworld."

Which could only mean one thing. "Amy?"

"Your mother wishes to take her slumber." He flicked his long fingers as though tossing the comment away, like it was meaningless. He'd just told me that my mother was ready to slumber, which basically translated to: she'd tired of life and wanted to die.

I hovered my glass near my lips, the shock enough to stall Osiris's compulsion. Ammit was a constant, like the sky or the earth. It had never crossed my mind that she'd step down. "When?"

"Well, these things take time, but time is a currency we gods have a surplus of." He bounced his bare foot. "She wishes to see you."

Which was easier said than done, since I was cursed to walk this earth by the very god I was currently drinking with.

I finally took the sip of wine, hiding my expression behind the glass. Something wasn't right. Osiris wouldn't go back on his curse and agree to let me visit the underworld to pay my respects. That was a kindness the god didn't have in him. Equally as suspicious, if it was that important, he could compel me to go home. Why give me the choice at all?

"She was a good mother to you," he said.

There wasn't a question there, so I didn't reply. Ammit wasn't my mother by blood, but she had taken me in and treated me like her own. They say that about the river beasts —vicious, but doting on their own kind. She was the ferocious Devourer of Souls, the final destination, and no god wanted to risk their paradise in the afterlife by crossing her— something I'd learned the hard way.

"I've always wondered why she took you in," Osiris said with a whimsical tone that had the fine hairs on the back of my neck rising. "A nameless nothing, like you. She likes to keep her secrets, your mother."

No more or less than any other god, I thought.

Osiris was looking at me, waiting for a reaction. He knew I couldn't do anything without his permission, and so we played this ancient game. His control. My obedience. "You must miss the old world as much as I do?"

I uselessly fought the compulsion, reluctant to give him anything he could use against me, but the answer came. "I do."

"I imagine it's the power you miss most ..."

Not a question. I kept my jaw locked.

"Is it? Tell me the truth."

"Yes." *Bastard.* This game, the strings he pulled and how he watched it all—every twitch, every glance, and every time I ground my teeth—was wearing me down. He poked and prodded me like an animal he'd caught in a trap, one he could torture for all eternity.

My gaze had strayed to the dagger and stayed fixed there, revealing my thoughts as plain as day. Of course, he'd noticed too and smiled when I forced myself to look him in the eye.

"If you wish to return, I'll sanction your passage."

Why? Why would he help me return home? What was in it for him? This wasn't right. I had to think this through and find his angle before I agreed to anything.

"You do wish to return?" he asked casually.

"Yes, and I'll consider it."

"What is there to consider?" His laughter, short, sharp, and dark, left me with no doubt that he was deliberately jerking my chain.

"I need to consider why you're giving me the choice," I growled, teeth gritted. My fingers itched to close around his neck and choke the life out of him. Such mundane actions couldn't kill gods and certainly not gods as powerful as Osiris. Still, it would feel good.

We locked gazes—a challenge—until I looked away, too afraid to see the truth inside those eyes.

He threw back his wine glass and downed its contents. "Isis, darling," he beckoned.

I watched the goddess in the corner of my eye. She drew the young woman from the bed and led her over. The girl had the wide-eyed, half-high look of someone godstruck. Get too close to a higher deity, like Isis, for too long, and their allure became intoxicating. After spending time with the pair, her mind was probably lost in a pleasurable numbness. I doubted she even remembered her name.

"Are you finished, my sweetness?" Osiris smiled up at his wife.

Isis leaned down, rode her hand up his neck, and kissed him deeply.

"Yes," she whispered against her husband's lips.

They looked into each other's eyes and power thrummed

in the air between them—the power of an eternity spent together and of the two most feared deities the worlds had ever seen.

"Good," Osiris said, and with his gaze firmly fixed on Isis, he added, "Nameless One, kill the girl."

CHAPTER 6

The water in the sink had turned pink. I dug under my nails to get every minuscule piece of dried blood out, but no matter how hard I scrubbed, there was always more. Steam bellowed, fogging up the mirror. At least I couldn't see my face, my eyes, my soul.

A few raps on the door rattled my scattered thoughts.

My gut heaved. I'd already emptied its contents behind Osiris's garage, but my stomach didn't seem to care. It carried on heaving, trying to eject the guilt.

I pulled the plug, twisted on the faucet, swirled water, rinsed off the pink splatters, and splashed my face. My fingers trembled, like the rest of me.

"Ace, open up or I'll kick it in."

I couldn't deal with Shu, not in the state I was in. I should have gone home, but the office was closer, and I hadn't expected her to notice my arrival. She usually went out of her way to avoid me.

"Whatever personal crisis you're having," she shouted through the closed door, "I don't give a shit. I'm gonna count to three. One, two—"

PIPPA DACOSTA

I wrenched the door open. "What?!"

She recoiled, just a fraction, and then her eyes darkened and her brow cut a jagged scowl. "You fucked up."

I laughed because it was all I had left. "You'll have to narrow it down."

Barging past her, I retreated to my office and dropped into my chair. I'd planned to check my emails, but I couldn't remember why. I had no problem recalling how blood looked in a crystal glass though. How it clung to the sides, thick and dark, almost black.

Shu wisely loitered in my doorway. If she came any closer, I'd likely hurl my letter opener at her.

"That job," she said. "The kids who summoned something nasty in midtown? Someone had a hobby telescope pointed at the rooftop."

A little static shock of magic fizzled through my fingers. The girl's soul had been light and made of brilliance—innocent but for a few dark smudges. Had I weighed her, I'd have found her worthy. She would have rested for all eternity in the afterlife, where she belonged. But I hadn't weighed her. She'd never gotten that chance.

"Ace!" Shu barked. "Did you hear me?"

She'd tasted sweet. I could feel the light in her still, feel it dancing at my fingertips, plucking on pleasure. My body buzzed with life, magic, power. It had been so long...so long... I'd held out. I'd resisted.

"You're wanted for questioning in connection with the murders of those three kids."

"Three?" I asked. There had been four.

"A fourth—Jason Montgomery—is missing," she said, as if reading my thoughts.

My mind sharpened, focus narrowing. "Does the PD have my name?"

"No, just a description. It's blown up on the internet: the

guy with the coat and sword. They're talking about you like you're some kind of vigilante bent on protecting the city from the rising dead."

They wouldn't say that if they knew I'd spent the morning washing off the blood of an innocent girl.

"You need to lay low. No more jobs. No more sword. Ditch the coat and wear a hat or something."

She *was* worried. Not for me, but for her own hide.

"I'll find the kid," I said. "He can tell the cops his pal went nuts and killed them all and then did himself in on the roof. He's terrified. He'll tell the cops what I tell him to tell them."

One of Shu's dark eyebrows crawled higher. "And the vigilante?"

"Urban legend. It was snowing. Whatever footage that's circulating, it'll be virtually indecipherable."

She considered it, but that scowl of hers wasn't getting any softer. "Let the cops find the kid."

I could let it go. It wasn't like I didn't already have enough on my mind, but I hated loose ends—like snakes, they tended to come back around and bite me in the ass—and Jason Montgomery was one hell of a loose end. At the very least, I needed to have a chat with him.

"Fine." Shu sighed, seeing the determination on my face and likely sensing now was not the time to argue. "Don't get caught. It's bad enough I have to spend every day working with you. I'd rather not be stuck in a prison cell with your righteous ass for the next fifty years."

"Feeling's mutual."

Find the kid. I turned my mind to that and forcibly denied that morning's events, pushing them way back where all the darkness of my past hid.

My cell chimed. I read Cujo's name and waved Shu away. "Hey, Cujo—"

"Funny thing. There's a video online of a guy in a long

coat with a badass broadsword. You wouldn't know anything about that?"

"Sounds like a freak." I grinned, grateful I could call Cujo a friend—one of few. "What kind of idiot carries a sword around New York?"

"Yeah, my thoughts exactly. Anyway, that's not why I'm calling. I looked into that bundle of joy of yours. Nineteen years old. She goes by the name *Chuck*."

"What kind of name is that?"

Cujo paused. "Do you want me to answer that? Apple doesn't fall far from the tree."

"I earned my nickname, same as you."

"I got my name because a crackhead bit me and I lost it. Tell me again how you got the name *Ace*?"

"Cheating at cards," I lied. He knew it was a lie too, which was why he kept asking. *Ace* didn't always have good connotations. Go back far enough, a few centuries, and it was another word for bad luck, or a curse. "Tell me about Chuck."

"No parents. She was abandoned at a firehouse as a six-month-old. In and out of foster homes since she was nine. A stint on the streets. She has herself a rap sheet for drug possession and theft, which was how I was able to trace her so fast."

As he talked, that niggling, little voice of truth chipped away at my denials. Cujo was right, the apple never fell far, and Chuck's background sounded all too familiar. "Cut to the chase, Cujo."

"Difficult to know if she's showing any unusual talents, but her name appears in the files of a few unresolved homicide cases. The victims were street douches. No witnesses. No charges. She was brought in but clammed up every time. Can't say homicide would have wasted much manpower there, but your girl could have been caught up in something that went sideways, and if she does have *talents*, that might be how some nasty folks got themselves dead. From what I hear, little godlings often make mistakes that end with people dying."

Ancient gods made mistakes too. I squeezed my eyes closed and pinched the bridge of my nose. A lot of things were my fault, but not this, not her. The girl's upbringing was all on Bast. I hadn't known about her. I didn't get the chance to help.

"Ace?"

"Uh-huh, still here."

"Short of a DNA test, I can't tell you much more."

"Do you know where she is?"

"There's a shelter in Queens. I'll email you the address. The shelter offers support for pregnant women in crisis."

"Okay, thanks, Cujo. Hey, the missing kid, Jason Montgomery. Let me know if you get any leads."

"Funny," he mock-whispered. "The sword guy, they say he can walk through Hell unburned."

I laughed. "It's not the fire that burns, my friend. It's the gods you gotta watch out for. Thanks for this, and I owe you one."

"I'm keeping tabs. You owe me at least fifty. But sure, why not? Gotta get my kicks somewhere. Stay safe, Ace."

CHAPTER 7

The snow in the street had turned to slush and refrozen in piles along the sidewalks outside the *Goddess of the Rising Sun Women's Shelter.* The name alone was a neon sign to anyone paying attention. Bast had many names, all the gods did, and this shelter was one of hers.

More people were filing through the doors than I'd expected. Inside, the staff served hot food and offered somewhere warm and dry for the cold and hungry to rest. I made my way through the line, quickly coming to the conclusion that blending in with roughly forty pregnant women wouldn't be easy.

"Can I help you?" A matronly woman stepped into my path. She was thin as a rake, gnarled like a tree, and had fierce eyes. She looked frail, but she'd bring out the claws if I threatened her or hers in any way.

"I'm looking for someone. A girl. Her name's—"

"Are you with the police?" She looked me over, suspicion in her words.

"No, I—"

"Then I can't tell you anything. As you can imagine, we

get a lot of men through these doors looking for their wives, daughters, friends. Our women are often here to get away from such men."

"I just—"

"I'm sorry, sir, but you'll have to leave."

"It's okay, Roseanne." Bast settled a hand on the woman's narrow shoulder. "I know him." She nodded at me. "I'll make sure he doesn't get into any trouble."

According to Cujo's recent information, I was already in trouble.

Bast led me to a quiet corner at the back of the hall, and before I could ask any of the questions bubbling in my head, she produced a list from her biker jacket pocket and handed it over. "There are many more women at risk. I've narrowed down the names to those who are pregnant and currently living in Manhattan."

I scanned the names. "I'm not here for them."

"Our daughter has my protection."

"That hasn't worked out too well for those who've already died."

She set her jaw and narrowed her finely lined dark eyes. "I can't be everywhere at once. The women on that list need *your* help."

Turning my back to Bast, I scanned the hall but couldn't see any girl I'd recognize as Chuck. I just wanted to see her. If I saw her, I'd know if she was my blood. Wasn't that how it worked with children? You just knew, as if there was a connection starting from the DNA out. "Where is she?"

"You believe me now?"

"I'm withholding judgment."

Her hand settled on my shoulder, and her fingers applied enough pressure to tempt me to face her. The last time she'd touched me—two decades ago—it had been with a slap across my face and a knee to my balls. I *had* deserved it, which was probably why it still hurt.

Her big, dark eyes looked apologetic. Bast never looked sorry. She was made of steel and reverence and had once been worshipped as the Great Protector. She didn't give an inch in anything, but these deaths had gotten to her. They undermined her strength like nothing else could. And looking into her eyes, I knew why. She'd once lost a legion of her most feared and revered warriors—four thousand women all under her protection. Trained by her, loved by her, and all slaughtered because of her allegiance during the last great sundering, when the old world had fallen and the gods lost their combined power.

"I didn't tell you," Bast said with a sigh, "because she's better off without us."

She was right, and it should have been that simple, but an irrational anger whipped through me, sweeping all reason aside. "It wasn't your choice to make alone."

The venom behind my words surprised me, and by Bast's widening eyes, her too. She hadn't expected me to care and neither had I.

"You were never supposed to know," she explained, saying it softly as though that might lessen the impact. "That's how it should have stayed."

I stepped in closer and lowered my voice. "Do you know the life she's had? She's been alone, on the streets, unwanted."

Bast bowed her head, sending her gaze through the floor. Her shoulders dropped, and I watched the fight fade from the eyes of the strongest woman I'd ever known.

"But it's a life." She leaned a shoulder against the wall, dislodging flakes of paint. "Nobody knows, Ace. If Osiris knew... What kind of life would she have had as a pawn among our kind?"

It didn't take much effort to recall how Osiris had flexed

his godly muscles with me. If he discovered I had a daughter, he'd have a whole new array of horrific ways to torture me, the girl, and Bast.

"She had a choice," Bast said, her voice regaining some of its steel. "Every day she has choices, and they're hers to make." She looked over the murmuring crowd. "Choice was the only gift I could give her."

Her words snagged at my heart, where a terrible weight clung. There was a soul-deep longing in my ex-wife's eyes. She'd given up her daughter, not because she didn't want her, but to keep her safe.

I followed Bast's far-eyed gaze through the crowd and over the heads of strangers until I found the girl at the end of the far table. She was hunched over her bowl of soup as though expecting someone to snatch it away from her. She had Bast's straight black hair, but Chuck's was messy, like she had cut it herself. Defined cheekbones gave her a fierce beauty, with lips that seemed too perfect to snarl. Her eyes though—even from across the hall I could see how her eyes entranced. Long, dark lashes around soul-seer eyes speckled with gold. She held the weight of the world in her eyes. To think she might have my power, the ability to see the worth of someone's soul and the terrible knowledge that came with it. Nineteen years old. Nineteen years was nothing. A blink. But her soul would already be old.

"She looks like her mom." My voice came out flat and disinterested and didn't reflect the turmoil raging inside.

"Not the eyes."

She's beautiful, I thought, but was her soul like her mother's or mine?

Bast had done the right thing. Chuck could never know about us or the rest of *everything*. My ex-wife had kept the truth from me, as we would now keep it from Chuck. She'd hate us for it. She'd rage that it wasn't our choice to make, that she deserved to know, and she'd be right. My first lesson in parenting: you can't win.

I looked down at the list of pregnant women Bast wanted me to protect. One name had a line scored through it.

"Her body was found last night," Bast explained.

"All right." I folded up the note and tucked it into my pocket. "But you and me need to talk. Not here. We—"

A hail of shouts erupted from across the hall. Bast launched into the crowd, her black-clad figure disappearing among the crush of fleeing people. I pushed forward, stepped up onto the nearest table, and saw Chuck dash out the door, followed by what looked like a large, pointed-eared Dober-man. Hopefully that's what all these witnesses would think—a dog attack. I knew otherwise. The jackals were search-and-destroy demons from my old neighborhood.

Behind the demon, a large liquid streak of black—vaguely resembling a big cat—followed. Bastet.

I jumped from tabletop to tabletop and skidded outside in time to see three figures carving their way down the side-walk. Chuck veered left, out of sight around a corner. The demon and Bast followed, seconds behind. Demons in broad daylight and I didn't have my sword. Just great.

I caught up with Bast—in her black-panther form—at the bottom of an extended fire escape ladder. Too bad big cats couldn't climb ladders. She circled, massive black paws padding in the filthy snow, and snuffled her nose against the slush, picking up the scent trail.

"I'm going up," I told her. "Stay out of sight."

She gave her glossy, black coat an all-over shake and planted her rump on the sidewalk, in full view of anyone who happened to turn down the street. There was no mistaking a black panther for a house cat.

"You sit there like that and animal control will be all over you."

She yawned, showing me perfect rows of man-eating teeth inside her skull-crushing jaw, and then rumbled some sort of "bring it" growl.

"Fine, get yourself noticed. I'll come see you when you're in the city zoo." I started up the ladder, followed by her low, bubbling growl.

Chuck was either smart or lucky. Climbing the fire escape had deterred the jackal, but it wouldn't stop it. They were excellent trackers. The beast was likely already finding another way into the building.

I climbed up a few flights and spotted drapes flapping from an open window.

"Chuck?" I hissed, sticking my head inside. Something large and black loomed to my right. I shot out a hand and caught the pan before it could crack my skull open.

Chuck's eyes flashed, and then she was off, dashing around a couch and heading for the door.

"Hey, wait. The dem—the dog—"

The door flung open and a hundred pounds of jackal demon slammed into Chuck, sending her sprawling. I lunged forward in time to see Chuck kick the jackal backward, across the wooden floor, and scrabble to her feet. That had taken some strength, the inhuman kind.

Inserting myself between jackal and girl, I brandished the pan and growled, "Think twice."

The jackal sank its claws into the timber floor and sprang. I swung and belted the pan across its muzzle with enough force to kill a man. It tumbled and whimpered but was on its feet in seconds, hollow eyes aflame and aimed at me.

Alysdair would have come in handy right about then. I could, of course, unleash the renewed magic bubbling in my veins, but that would require a lot of explaining. As things stood, a few lies about an escaped exotic wolf from the city zoo would explain most of the events so far. If I spouted spells, Chuck would ask questions I wasn't ready to answer.

The jackal's lips rippled over vicious teeth. It lowered its head and planted one forepaw forward and then the other.

I focused my gaze. "You clearly don't know who you're messing with."

Its pointed ears flattened against its head.

Chuck ran for the door and the jackal hunched to launch after her.

I saw my chance, kicked the door closed, and flung out my left hand. "*Hurzd!*" *Hold!*

The demon's approached stalled. It whipped its head up and recognition sparked in its rippling eyes. Down went its haunches and its head, until its belly touched the floor. Shame softened its so-sorry eyes, as if I'd come home to find my couch and slippers all chewed up.

"It's too late for that."

I tossed the pan aside, curled the fingers of my outstretched hand closed, and whispered old words. They tumbled from my lips—no pauses, no respite—and as they built, power trembled through my body, rekindling old urges. Without Alysdair, I was out of options. This was the only way.

The jackal started whimpering again. It had been years since I'd spoken the spell. Today I'd wielded the magic twice, and the day wasn't over yet.

'Tra k-dae amcru-kak sra ksork, kosec amcru-kak esk kass-rakamsk, omd kae kuir amcru-kak aeuirk." The sky encloses the stars, magic encloses its settlements, and my soul encloses yours.

The ancient words sounded harsh and guttural, the language forgotten by all but the oldest of us.

My eyes locked with the jackal's and pinned it, leaving it quivering in its own piss. The words lost their form but not their meaning. I dug deeper into the beast's eyes, the spell spiraling between us, and deeper into the writhing darkness that made up its soul. Its spirit fought, black talons slicing, and distantly it screamed its death wail, but the soul was mine.

"By the grace of Amun-Ra." The words trembled. Magic surged. "By the power invested in me, by the sire Osiris, by the light, the dark, I have weighed your soul. You are encumbered. The Devourer accepts your eternal spirit as recompense."

The words hooked in, and there was no escape. I wrenched the fetid black soul free of its earthly grip. The darkness barreled into me, over me, spilling through my physical body, and flowed deeper until the hunger in me rose and enclosed it all, embracing the dark.

The jackal collapsed.

I dropped and rocked on my knees, head buzzing, my thoughts strewn about, impossible to reorder. The demon's final soul scream echoed into nothingness.

"Daquir." Devour.

The word of power had barely pushed off my lips before the jackal's earthly body burst into a puff of ash and embers. Gone for eternity. Not of this life or the next. The ultimate punishment.

Bast—in human form—kicked the door in, saw me on my knees, and sniffed at the air. She'd smell the ash and know exactly what had happened here.

"You all right?" she asked.

"Will be," I ground out, still swimming through the fog in my head. "Go find her. If there's one jackal, there'll be others."

She hesitated, and a smile touched my lips. I didn't know she cared.

"Go."

"You didn't have to do this," she said.

"I did." I reached for the back of the couch and hauled myself onto unsteady legs. "Go, Bast. Call me when she's safe."

I watched her go and let out a sigh that sounded too much like a lover's gasp. Alone, with the remnants of the spell and the fragments of a broken soul dancing through me, I lifted my gaze and smiled.

CHAPTER 8

I'd added Bast's cell to my contacts and attributed the most fitting song to her ringtone I could find. So when The Cure's "The Love Cats" trilled from my cell, I knew exactly who was calling. She told me she'd found Chuck and was taking her out for a bite to eat, hoping to get more information out of her.

I met the pair of them at one of those fancy bars that couldn't decide if it was a restaurant or a watering hole. Nineteen-forties chandeliers hung from high ceilings, black and white prints adorned the walls, and servers darted between tables with sliders on slates. I figured it was Bast's favorite haunt and ordered the only thing on the menu I could afford —a black coffee—and dumped a ton of sugar in it.

Chuck looked at me through narrowed, darting eyes, suspicion radiating off her. I'd seen that look in wild cats, the ones that scratched the hand trying to help them. She was too pale, and up close, I wondered if her sharp features had more to do with malnourishment than godly genes.

"You're the guy from the apartment," she said by way of hello.

"You're welcome."

"Chuck, this is Ace. He's a friend," Bast replied, giving me a furtive look that probably meant something, but I had no idea what.

"You going to eat that?" Chuck asked Bast, nodding at the goddess's scraps.

I'd arrived late, and the two of them had almost finished their meals. Without a word, Bast switched plates with Chuck, who quickly began vacuuming up the remains.

"What was that thing?" Chuck asked me around a mouthful of burger bun.

I flicked a questioning gaze at Bast.

"Wild dog," she replied on my behalf. "It escaped from the zoo."

Chuck snorted. "Uh-huh, and I'm the pope's daughter."

She gulped half her lemonade in one go and looked right at me again, her gaze trawling over my face but avoiding my eyes. *Clever girl.*

Done with her visual interrogation, she slumped back in her seat and raked her ringed fingers through her short hair.

"Did you kill it?" she asked me.

Killed it, devoured it—same thing. "It's gone."

Chuck nodded appreciatively. "I've been running from those things for weeks, so why don't you two cut the Good Samaritan act and tell me what's really going on?"

"Bast?" I asked, handing the baton over before she could do the same to me.

Chuck twisted in her seat to look Bast over. The goddess had toned down her allure and hidden her cat-like eyes behind a small human illusion, but that didn't detract from her unusually striking appearance or her casual, but lethal elegance.

"I'm going to ask you some questions," Bast replied. "They may seem strange."

"Strange? Like a wild dog chasing me down the street? And that wasn't the only thing after me. I saw a cat. A big one. I swear it. I only caught a glimpse when I climbed the ladder, but it was real."

Silence descended over our table. I played with my spoon.

"I'm not nuts," Chuck added. "I know what I saw."

"You're pregnant—" Bast began.

"So? Everyone at that shelter is." She crossed her arms and glared at the goddess, daring an ageless Egyptian deity to judge her.

I hid my smile by tasting my sweet coffee.

"Who's the father?" Bast asked calmly.

Chuck shrugged. Her gaze flicked back to me and then down at her empty plate. She wouldn't answer anything, and I couldn't blame her. She didn't know us. She'd survived on the streets by her wits alone, and that meant not trusting anyone. I knew what that felt like. It was difficult to let people in after guarding yourself against them for what felt like forever. That was one of the reasons I'd only had the one friend in the last few decades.

"We're here to help," I said.

"Great. Got any cash? That'll help."

"What are you going to spend it on?" I asked.

"Louis Vuitton handbags and getting my nails done like Goth lady here. What do you think I'm going to spend it on?"

"Drugs?"

She clamped her mouth shut and folded her arms across her chest. "I don't do that no more. I'm clean."

"I know what addiction is," I said, avoiding Bast's pertinent look. "Tough to beat on your own."

"Well, I don't got nobody, so just give me the money and you can go back to your cozy little life knowing you did your good deed for the day."

"The dogs will come again," Bast butted in, sounding like a portent of doom. Goddesses and their drama.

Chuck bounced her teenage glare between us. "You won't tell me what's really going on here, so what's left to talk about?"

Bast shared another beseeching look with me but our wordless conversations clearly weren't helping.

"Chuck," Bast said, her voice tipping toward authoritative. "There may be other women like you. Women in trouble."

"More escaped dingoes, huh?"

I almost corrected her, but now both women were looking at me with varying degrees of contempt. Bast needed my help explaining, which, so far, I'd failed at, and Chuck knew it was all BS.

"I'm not telling you anything until you tell me the truth. You two talk it out. I'm going to the rest room." Chuck shuffled from the booth and strode to the back of the bar with the long-legged, powerful stride of a caged tiger. Chuck had more of her mother in her than looks alone. That was an uncomfortable thought. She clearly didn't know about shapeshifting, but she would learn fast if she developed that curious gift from her mother.

I grinned. "She's got sass."

Bast rolled her eyes at me. "It's all posturing. She's scared." She tapped her painted nails on the tabletop. "I need to find out where she's been, who she's been talking to, and who her friends are. There must be something."

"Good luck with that."

"You could help."

"She won't talk to us."

"We could tell her—"

"No," I cut her off. "You were right. The less contact we have with her, the more chance she has at having normal a life. If you mention gods, she'll think you're nuts, but she won't forget it. Then she'll start digging and connect the dots, and the picture she'll draw will come back to bite her. Happens every time. People can't help but poke at the unknown, and then it pokes back and gets them killed." *Or crippled for life,* I finished mentally, thinking of Cujo and the many others whose paths I'd crossed over the years.

"And if she has the magic?" Bast whispered. "What then? We're just going to let her flounder like an unclaimed godling?"

I winced and glared at my black coffee. Looking at Chuck was too much like looking in a mirror, but she could still escape her fate.

"She'll make a mistake," Bast said. "Osiris will notice. He'll kill her."

"If she's lucky," I mumbled.

Bast's dark brows shot up and I regretted the words. Sure enough, Bast read the weight in them. She knew about my curse, but not all of it. Not the details. *Seth ek em sra dasoerk. The devil is in the details.*

Bast rested an arm on the table, leaning in and making damn sure I had to look at her. "You didn't have to devour that demon."

"Yes, I did."

"When was the last time *you* devoured? Not the sword, *you?*"

"This morning, actually." And I was still coming down from that one.

She recoiled the way I had known she would and lifted her lip in a disgusted snarl. "If Osiris learns—"

"Osiris—" I stopped myself, aware I'd raised my voice along with my heart rate. "Bast, back off. I'm dealing with it."

"'Dealing with it'?" She snorted a judgmental laugh. "I was right. You haven't changed at all."

I wanted to lay into her, to tell her how Osiris knew I was devouring souls because he was the one who'd broken my abstinence, but what good would it do? She wouldn't believe me, and even if she did, there was nothing she could do. But she'd try and get herself tangled up in my mess. It would be easier for everyone if we all continued to believe what we wanted to. *Liar. Thief.*

"Let's address the Sphinx in the room, shall we?" I said.

She side-eyed me.

"The jackals. Few gods have dominion over them."

"Ammit traditionally controls them," she confirmed.

"Can you think of any reason why she'd want to attack your blessed?"

"None. I've never crossed Ammit." She shivered. "No sane god would."

A sane god? Somehow I kept from laughing. "If it isn't her, she'll know more. Osiris told me my mother wants to take her slumber. He said he'd sanction my return to the underworld."

Bast considered my words in silence. The sounds of people talking and laughing continued on around us, wrapping us in normalcy. I often forgot I wasn't part of their world, not even after all the years I'd walked among them. I would never belong, even though I'd done my damnedest to fit in once I'd stopped pining for home.

"You're going back?" Bast asked.

"I have to." I'd have been lying if I said the thought of going home didn't fill me with dread, as well as a deep, illicit thrill.

"How long has it been?" The compassion on her face and the regret in her eyes almost broke me down and had me telling her everything.

I remembered the white feather settling, the scales tipping, my heart falling, and the sounds of my own spell, spoken by Osiris, wrapping around me, through me, and binding my soul. The accusing eyes, the howls and screams from those I'd condemned—I remembered it all like it was yesterday. "Five hundred years, give or take a few."

Bast reached across the table and closed her warm, smooth hand around mine. Gooseflesh lifted the fine hairs on my arms and up my neck. I'd have liked to pull her in, close my arms around her, and hide. It had always worked before.

"You'll be okay."

My lips twitched in a mockery of a smile that didn't last. I pulled my hand from hers. "I always am."

I told Bast to look out for Chuck, which I didn't need to say but seemed like a decent enough goodbye, and left her alone at the table. Her gaze rode my back until I left the bar, but guilt clung to me, weighing me down with every step.

CHAPTER 9

Heat beat at me when I stepped from the mansion into the greenhouse—a vast indoor tropical garden easily the size of the main house. Exotic butterflies flitted around, fans gently circulated the air, and occasionally the *drip-drip* of water tapped on large leaves.

I yanked off my coat and undid a few shirt buttons. The heat wasn't my only problem; I'd devoured two souls in less than twenty-four hours. One dark and heavy, the other light and clean. Loosely translated, the immense magical high was twisting into a crippling comedown. And here I was about to have a voluntary talk with Osiris. I'd have preferred to wait a few days until the aftereffects had stabilized, but a few days could have meant the slaughter of more of Bast's women. I had enough darkness in my putrid soul without adding that.

"Nameless One..." Isis's slippery voice curled through the jungle foliage and brought me to an abrupt stop on the winding path.

"By Isis, all that has been, that is, or shall be; no mortal man hath ever unveiled." The proper greeting fell off my tongue as flat and empty as the countless times I'd said it before and would again.

She emerged from behind the large leaves of a tropical fern, trailing her fingers along its edges and lifting her traditionally kohl-accented eyes to mine in a way that had a small skitter of nerves shortening my breath.

"There are no mortal men here. Would you like to unveil me?"

There's no right way to answer a goddess—ever. Whatever I said next would be the wrong thing. If I said yes, she'd have me flailed for lusting after her divine body. If I declined, she'd be offended and would probably make me spend the next six months telling her how I did, in fact, lust after every inch of her. And that was if she was feeling generous.

Fucking gods.

"I'm here for Osiris."

"Mm..." She pulled the leaf with her and then let it fall away as she approached. "I didn't know you preferred the male form?"

Well, that was one way of escaping her word trap. But as she came forward, her slip of a gown parted up her thigh, revealing a trail of studded gems, and by Sekhmet, I made the mistake of imagining how I might follow that trail with my fingers and mouth. I clamped my teeth together and steered my thoughts away from dangerous territory, only to have them land on her lips and how she might taste beneath my tongue.

Those soft lips lifted at a corner.

"No, it is not men you prefer," she said, stopping too close to me. Her fingertips touched my thigh and then her nails raked higher. "No need for words, Nameless One." She found what she was looking for and pressed in, eliciting a sharp inhale from me. "I have my answer right here."

"Stop." I hadn't meant to add the compulsion—it was

pointless, of course—and all it did was widen the pupils of her eyes, as though she got off on my pathetic effort to control an eternal being like her.

"We could fuck right here, against this tree. I'd bend for you." With her alarmingly hot hand still resting on my arousal, she used her free hand to pluck at my shirt buttons. "You despise my husband. Wouldn't this be a fine way to hurt him?"

Oh, it would. She was painting a very fine image, one that I struggled to sweep from my thoughts, which had currently funneled right to where her hand was resting. Screwing Isis appealed to the part of me that had never truly left the underworld, the being I'd been before, a creature of power and want, worthy of fear and worship. That part of me had no trouble imagining how the Goddess of Light would taste, or how she'd feel bent over with my hands on her hips as I pounded into her. But it wouldn't last. She'd tell Osiris a patchwork of lies, and as perilous and exhilarating as screwing the goddess Isis would be, it wouldn't be worth the centuries of fallout her husband would rain down on me.

"I know what you're thinking," she whispered. Her breath fluttered across my lips. "But what else could he possibly do to you that he hasn't already done?"

I caught her hand, the one cupping my cock. "*Stop.*"

This time I pushed more weight behind the word. I'd devoured two souls in a few hours. Surplus magic was something I had in swathes.

Her beautiful eyes widened in alarm. I released her hand and watched her briefly war with the compulsion. It lasted a grand total of two seconds before it broke.

With a gasp, she stepped back. "How dare you!"

"You seem to have forgotten where I came from, Your Highness. I'm glad I could help you with that unfortunate mistake."

Color flushed her cheeks and fury flashed as hard and fast as lightning in her eyes. I didn't think for one second I'd escaped her wrath, but to see her taste some of her own poison brightened my day immeasurably.

If my soul wasn't already cursed, my actions would have earned one. I smiled and meant it. "Please inform your husband I'm here."

She left, striding down the path and out of sight. I waited until I was sure she was gone before slumping against the tree and gulping down several shuddering breaths. One god down, one to go.

Needing to set my mind on something other than my neglected cock, I roamed the garden, walking the winding paths beneath heavy palm fronds and around deep-throated exotic flowers.

Outside, snow patted lightly at the glass. With its heat and damp, earthy richness, I understood why the couple might like the gardens. The greenhouse smelled like the old world after the rains, when the Nile would flood, bringing much needed sustenance to the riverbanks. The people would revel in the sudden flourish of color and life, in celebrations of rebirth and festivals of plenty, giving thanks to the all-powerful gods for their generosity. Those had been joyous days and nights, but all that had changed when the gods grew bored and turned inward, allowing the worst of them to rise. Seth. The rains had stopped. The floods had failed. Crops had wilted under the relentless sun. And while the gods warred and bickered, Seth had cast his shadow over the land, the people had faded into dust, and the desert sand had devoured what had once been the greatest civilization on Earth.

I would often walk the riverbanks, running my hands through the miles and miles of wheat. I'd watched the children with baskets around their necks, singing as they scattered seeds. Occasionally, I'd join them and their families, never revealing who I was and keeping my power wrapped close. Though I had never belonged among them, I didn't care, not then. I'd spend evenings admiring the sailboats, listening to the slosh of oars, and watching, admiring, and living a normal life through the wonder of normal people.

But those memories were distant, like dreams, stories, myths. Today, those long-dead people and their fevered worship meant nothing. The gods were gone, relegated to religious texts and the occasional website selling fake protection spells. Now the gods, once so feared and revered, were confined to academia or the awe-filled eyes of tourists filing through barren tombs and crumbled temples.

The man who I had been *before*, he was dust and dreams. Perhaps he always had been.

I pulled up suddenly as Osiris jogged down the green-house steps, dressed in a tux and holding a cell phone to his ear. The image clashed so acutely with my memories that I forgot about the curse and my blind hatred of him and saw him how he had once been: the greatest of gods, worshiped and admired by his people as well as his pantheon. Armies had marched in his name. He was the god of all things. Life and death had played out inside his hands—decay and rebirth.

"I know... I'll be there. I don't care when the cameras are rolling. I will be there when I am ready. They'll wait."

Where had it all gone so wrong?

He hung up the call and frowned at my presence. "What by Sekhmet did you say to my wife?"

"Only that which she asked of me," I answered, avoiding the truth as best as I could, given his ability to extract answers out of me.

That didn't appease him. I hadn't really expected it to.

"She's in a foul mood and I have a gala I'm due to attend with her at my side. You have no idea what it's like."

I could imagine being married to Isis was a lot like sleeping in a bed of snakes: exhilarating, until it wasn't.

"I'd like to visit my mother," I said, veering the conversation away from Isis.

His smile was all perfect teeth. "Ah, yes, of course. I thought you might." He half turned but hesitated, and then slowly, purposefully, he slid his gaze back to me. "There are some conditions."

My heart sank.

"You should join us at the gala. We can talk more there."

I forced what I hoped looked like a smile on my lips and not a sneer. "I'm not dressed for fine dining."

"I'll soon change that." He turned, clicked his fingers, and said, "Come."

I plodded after him, trailing behind the god like a slave on an invisible chain that I'd keenly felt for five interminably long centuries.

⚜

IF THE UNDERWORLD WAS MY HOME, A CHARITY GALA WAS my idea of hell. Smiling faces, fake laughs, chinking glasses, and every word a weapon wielded for social ambition. I did my best to smile back and muster through painful small talk while the space between my shoulder blades itched for Alysdair's weight. I recognized a few faces from the orgy beneath Osiris's house. Thankfully those faces didn't recognize me all scrubbed up in a tux.

"Poison" blared from my cell phone, and probably for the first time in my life, I was grateful for Shu. Excusing myself from yet another conversation regarding politics, I stepped behind the table of canapés and hid away in a corner.

"Shu, kill me now," I growled.

"Where are you?"

"In hell."

She paused. "You're not, are you?"

I sighed, tucked a hand in my pocket, and slumped against the wall. "They don't have cell reception in the Hall of Judgment."

She grumbled a curse. "Did you get anywhere with the Montgomery kid?"

"Cujo will let me know if he gets any leads."

"Okay..."

"Why?"

"I think we might have a bigger problem than a scared kid."

The way the last few days had been going, I couldn't have been less surprised. "Are you going to keep it to yourself or share with the class?"

"Did you get a look at the spell they were casting?"

"Yeah, as accurate and deadly as they come."

"Did you keep it?" She didn't bother to hide the intrigue in her voice. Once a sorceress, always a sorceress.

"No, I didn't keep it. I burned it so you couldn't get your claws on it." It hadn't even crossed my mind to burn it to keep it from Shu, but I liked the idea, and her resulting hiss. I chuckled. "It was too potent. The kids didn't need to know the language. The fact it was there, inside their circle, was enough to bring the demon through."

"Demons."

"What?"

"I saw an interview with the Montgomery mother. Her son looked sick before he vanished. The press is trying to blame it on drugs. You know what they're like. They love a good socialite drug drama."

A second demon? It was possible. The demon—or

demons—had possessed their hosts before I arrived. I could have missed one, especially if it had buried itself so deep its host hadn't been aware of it. "Damn it."

"It's been over twenty-four hours. It would have turned him by now. Get your ass on this with a bit more urgency."

"I can't. I'm having canapés with Osiris." I deliberately omitted the part where women were dying and I needed to get to the underworld to find out why, just to get a rise out of Shu.

"For fuck's sake."

It worked.

A compulsion speared into me, yanking my head up, and there was Osiris, eyes fixed on me from across the room.

"Wherever the demon is, it's laying low," I said. "I gotta go. I'll get on it when I get back from Amy's. You deal with it."

"What? Amy's. Why—"

"I gotta go."

"You bastard. You better come back."

"I will."

"It's my ass on the line too—"

I hung up the cell, already moving at a brisk pace through the throng of people toward the smiling mayor. I *would* be back. I had to come back. Bast, the dying women, Chuck, and now the loose demon—they were loose ends, all of them. I couldn't leave them hanging.

"Ace, sit," Osiris ordered.

I pulled out the chair beside him and sat like a good puppet.

"Who was on the call?" he asked.

"Shukra."

One of Osiris's dark eyebrows jerked higher. "You two getting along?"

"Does a viper get along with a scorpion?"

"Which are you?"

I frowned, wishing I'd kept quiet. "Scorpion, obviously. Can we get to the conditions you mentioned?"

His laugh grated like nails on a chalk board. "So eager to get away. Why don't you enjoy the company and the wine?"

I'd have preferred to spend the evening with a demon, and considering what had happened the last time I'd shared a glass of red with Osiris, I really didn't want to relive those memories or the experience.

"The conditions?" I asked, doing my best to look innocent to anyone who happened to be glancing at the mayor. He drew the eyes of many. Me sitting next to him was already damaging what reputation I had in my small world of clients.

"Yes..." He breathed in deeply through his nose and leaned a little closer while his gaze roamed the sea of happy, sparkly rich people. "I'm convinced my wife is having an affair."

My memory flashed to the image of his wife's hand on my cock. *Guilty, guilty, guilty,* my heart thudded. I shifted in my seat and cleared my throat. "Oh?"

An older gentleman arrived and rained compliments down on the mayor. How delightful it was to have such a proactive young mayor running the city. He'd had his doubts, in the beginning, but Ozzy had turned the city around.

I squirmed as Osiris smiled, accepted the compliments with grace, and shook the gentleman's hand.

While they talked, I wondered what Osiris considered an affair. They'd both been screwing the unfortunate girl when I'd seen them together yesterday. Where did the god draw the line? More to the point, what the hell would he ask of me? I couldn't investigate Isis. She'd tie me up in knots. I knew my limitations. Getting between Isis and Osiris was tantamount to suicide.

The gushing praise faded and the gentleman went away,

ruddy cheeked and happy. Osiris chuckled and tasted his wine. "So easily pleased."

"Isis," I said, determined not to spend the night dancing to Osiris's tune.

His smile faded. He spied his wife weaving through the crowd like a snake through the grass. Her green evening gown flowed over her body like emerald liquid. She'd pinned her hair up, twisted it into knots, and planted jewels inside the design. Whichever way she turned, people stopped her, their eyes alight with adoration. She *was* stunning and made a man forget his thoughts, his vows, his honor. She could have anyone.

She turned her head, sensing Osiris's gaze on her, and shared a private smile with her husband. She ignored me, thankfully.

"*She's fucking Thoth*," Osiris said, his voice cutting deep into my thoughts. He hadn't spoken aloud, and even now he smiled back at his wife.

I spluttered. "The lawyer?"

"How many Thoths do you know?" Osiris drawled.

Thoth was perfectly suited to a life of litigation and numbers. I'd never seen him wearing anything other than a charcoal gray suit, and I'd only seen him crack a smile once. He was as rigid and unyielding as stone. The thought of him and Isis together? That just didn't seem likely. Maybe he was an animal in the bedroom. We all had our hidden talents.

"She's been...distant," Osiris confided, watching the crowd swallow Isis. "We've had our challenges."

I could imagine. Seven thousand years as husband and wife would take its toll. Then there was the fact that they were also brother and sister. Relationships didn't get more complicated than that.

"Isis is"—he swallowed—"insatiable, and I too may have been distracted as of late." Osiris shifted in his chair and poured the dregs from a bottle of champagne into his glass. "She's been meeting with him in secret."

He lifted the glass and continued watching the crowd, avoiding looking directly at me.

"Do you have proof of the affair?"

"That's what I need you for."

Great, someone shoot me now. Marital grievances were bad enough without adding all-powerful deities to the drama. To make matters worse, Thoth was Amun-Ra's son. As gods went, Thoth could rip me a new one in a blink. I'd stayed below the radar of most godly goings-on, but getting between Osiris, Isis, and Thoth? There wasn't any way I was coming out of that fire unburned.

"What sort of proof?" I asked, thoughts churning.

"All of it. If Thoth is touching my wife, I want every detail, every word, so I can make him eat his treachery."

Treachery wouldn't be the only thing Osiris would force Thoth to eat. If he could confine Thoth to the underworld, Osiris would have significant power over him. A clash between titans like that would ripple through the entire pantheon, and such an upheaval hadn't happened since the end of the old world. A civilization had fallen then. There was no telling what might fall this time—and I'd be right in the middle of it.

I needed a drink. I waved a server over and took a glass of wine. Osiris hadn't compelled me to work for him. He could, so why wasn't he?

"There's more, isn't there?" I asked.

Osiris blinked and looked at me as though he were surprised. "Of course. Once you have proof, you will kill Thoth."

I choked on my wine, spilling much of it over my fingers and onto my lap. *He's insane.*

I laughed, flicked the wine from my fingers, and dabbed at

my pants with a napkin. He had to be joking. I couldn't kill Thoth. If I were capable of killing gods, I'd have killed Osiris long ago.

Osiris wasn't smiling and an icy shiver trickled down my back. He'd told me to kill Thoth. His words should have compelled me, but I didn't feel any different. I didn't feel the urge to pick up Alysdair and go god hunting.

Had his compulsion failed? "You'd have a better chance at killing Thoth than me. I'm just a mercenary without a name."

"I cannot strike a direct blow at Thoth. Such an act would start a political collapse. I have no wish to destabilize everything I've worked so hard to construct. This realm and our place in it, it is all about to change. I cannot risk millennia of planning because my wife is screwing another."

I absorbed that information and carefully packed it away for later consideration. "I can't kill a god, Osiris."

Godkiller was not a title I'd survive.

Osiris pursed his lips. His long fingers teased the rim of his glass. "I cannot compel you to do this. Thoth's power rivals mine and no compulsion would stand the weight of a task such as this one. But I will lift a condition of your curse. You'll be free to return home whenever you wish. Your mother can rest well in the afterlife knowing she has seen you. I am aware of some pertinent confessions she'd like to share with you before her slumber."

Kill Thoth and this realm would no longer be a prison.

Clearly Osiris believed I was capable, even if I didn't. That information alone was worth keeping close to my chest. In order to get back to the underworld, help Bast, her women, and Chuck, and see my mother again before she passed on, I had to agree to kill a god. If I succeeded, and that was a monumental *if*, I'd reduce the curse strangling my soul, but I'd also have the knowledge that Osiris had ordered me to kill a god—knowledge I could use against Osiris.

Knowledge powerful enough to keep my daughter safe should any god come looking?

This was a dangerous proposition, one I wasn't entirely sure I could survive.

"I agree," I said and then gulped down the last of my wine in one shot. "Lift the realm lock now."

Osiris's dark eyes flashed with warning, and something else, something like mischief. I already regretted my decision, but I couldn't see any other way out of this. He'd never allow me to say no.

"It will be done."

Osiris stood. Several people glanced our way over their wine glasses. They couldn't help themselves. The entire room was probably halfway in love with him. Given a few more hours, he could have them all enthralled and probably lining up to join him below his house.

"Come," he said, paying his rapt audience no mind.

Isis's intense glare was the last thing I saw in the crowd before I followed her husband out of the room.

CHAPTER 10

Osiris uttered the spellword, *hurzd,* blocking the men's restroom door from any unwanted intruders, and wasted no time starting the curse reversal. He rinsed his hands, and while his fingers dripped water, he placed both palms on my cheeks. "Close your eyes."

I did, with relief.

"Bruud uk kema, kur sros vrecr aeui roqa baam birdam," His eternal power flexed in the room, swelling outward, and then snapped back with a pressurized pop. *"Koae muv reka."*

I didn't feel any different when it was done. As was the way with magic, you generally didn't notice it until it was too late. "How do I know it'll work?"

Osiris simply smiled, dug into his tuxedo's pocket, and handed over two battered bronze coins. "Give the ferryman my regards."

He turned to leave.

I closed my hand around the warm coins. "When I do this..."

He paused at the door, his back to me. We both knew I

wasn't talking about the trip back home, but the deal I'd struck. *Godkiller.*

"I'll have your protection from the pantheon?"

His shoulders straightened into a solid line. "You already do."

The door clicked closed behind him, leaving me standing alone beneath the buzzing fluorescent lights. My reflection frowned back at me, concern and doubt etched into my face. "Yeah, I know. What else was I supposed to do?"

No time like the present. Filling one of the sinks to the brim, I shrugged off my borrowed jacket, rolled up the shirtsleeves, and plunged both hands into the water.

"Ovam kur ka, kur I ok uk sra oer, sra aorsr, sra resrs, omd sra dord. Ovam omd varcuka ka srruisr." Open for me, for I am of the air, the earth, the light, and the dark. Open and welcome me through.

The lights flickered, and that was the only sign I'd get. Opening a door to the underworld wasn't all that dramatic. No flaming doorways or blinding light. Old magic knew how to hide.

My amber-glittered eyes glowed a little too brightly in the mirror. I reached out my fingers and dabbed at the glass. Ripples shivered across the surface.

Five hundred years was a long time to walk this earth. A long time in which much could have changed back home. I hadn't left on the best of terms.

I gripped the sink's edge and peered into my reflection. I had changed. I hadn't had much choice in that, but I was ready to go home. Wasn't I?

Draining the water, I climbed onto the counter and pushed through the mirror.

For the longest moment, the crossing between realms felt like being submerged in warm water. The weight pushed in, not just against my skin and clothes, but into my mind. For a few seconds, it felt like I was drowning. There was no right way up, no sky, no ground, no sound, and no taste—until I opened my eyes and took my first breath. And there it was, the plaza. I hesitated, grounding myself.

Massive pillars held aloft a vast portico over the entrance to the Hall of Judgment, and all around pointed temples stretched into the distant, never-ending glare. The air smelled sweet, like honey, and the breeze was soft, warm, familiar, and welcoming.

Duat. Home sweet home. It had been too long.

Power buzzed beneath my skin, coming alive in my realm, and lent me a radiance I didn't deserve. I'd spent so long in the dark that this world and its brilliance scorched.

Figures drifted in my peripheral vision, the Hall spirits. They'd remain little more than dust motes in sunlight until they wanted to show themselves. I felt their curiosity pushing at me. If they sensed weakness, they wouldn't be nearly as benevolent. I strode on, sweeping through their numbers in my mortal clothing: black pants and black shirt, so black against the light. Fitting, perhaps.

I climbed the Hall's steps. Cracks had split some, and others had crumbled. I didn't remember them being so neglected. Pausing at the top, I noticed other faults in the buildings around me. Corners were whittled away and capping stones were dislodged, while some had crumbled into ruins. Yes, much had changed.

Whispers floated on the breeze. *Liar. Thief. Soul Eater,* those whispers said. They were right, and the truth of it pushed down, weighting my steps and my heart even more.

The doors creaked open, and a towering burial-wrapped statue of Osiris met me. Easily five stories high, there were smaller buildings in New York. The statue was meant as a statement. Even in his absence, Osiris ruled. The crook and flail crossed against his chest were larger than my entire apartment. Feeling reduced, as was the point, I walked around the monolith and through an equally tall, narrow corridor. Hieroglyphs covered the floor, the walls, the ceiling. I reached a hand out and ran my fingertips over the colorful displays.

"*Rarru.*" *Hello*. The word sailed into vacant spaces, seeking the familiar.

Raku, I heard echo back. *Home*.

On the hallway stretched, and on I walked, passing by the depictions of epic battles, wars, victories, and defeats, all chiseled into the walls and painted in a riot of color. These halls were a celebration of life and death and how one was irrevocably tied to the other.

I couldn't slow. If I slowed, I'd linger. If I lingered, I'd get comfortable.

I can't stay. This had once been my home, but now...now it was something else, somewhere I no longer belonged.

I dragged my feet but kept moving and emerged inside the flooded crossing chamber, where a small wooden sailboat bobbed against its mooring. The hooded ferryman held out his cotton-wrapped fingers.

"Osiris sends his regards," I said, dropping one coin into his palm.

I assumed the ferryman was male, though as far as I knew, nobody had ever seen his true face. There was no face beneath the hood, and no body beneath the robe—just the spirit knotted among its burial wrappings.

He made what sounded like a distinct chuckle and beckoned me aboard. The boat rocked under my weight but settled, and we pushed silently into the fog.

"It is good...you are here." His whispers were as insubstantial as the mist we drifted through.

I peered over the edge of the boat and saw hollow-eyed faces flicker in and out of focus beneath the water's surface. These waters were sacrosanct. I'd once—as a boy—swam with the souls. It was a secret only the ferryman knew and one that would likely add to my hefty rap sheet of sins should Osiris ever discover it.

"Many years have passed," the ferryman said.

I wet my lips, tasting the mist and the whispers. "*Seka kreak.*" *Time flies.*

I'd left in disgrace, but in the underworld, only my mother knew the real reason I couldn't return. The spirits of the underworld and the demon gods would assume, of course, that I'd been afraid to return. That might have been true for the first few centuries—and might still be true, if my trembling fingers were to be believed.

Another chuckle. "Your mother, weary she is."

I leaned forward, resting my elbows on my knees, and ran my fingers through my mist-soaked hair. "I'm sorry for that."

"The Great Devourer speaks of regret."

And so she should. It was one thing to banish your son, and another to hand him over to Osiris. I knew punishment, and that sentence did not fit my crimes.

Dragging a hand down my face to clear the memories, I peered over the ferryman's shoulder into the fog. Massive columns rose out of the nothingness, reaching like mountain-tops through the clouds. Like Osiris's statue, the Temple of Light towered higher and farther than anything manmade. Even the gods were reduced to ants inside its walls. A wary warmth spread throughout my chest. Whatever happened, whatever I'd done, whatever I was about to do for Osiris, I was glad my path had brought me home.

The ferry gently nudged the steps. I thanked the ferryman, sparing his hooded face a smile, and jogged up the steps. The heavy doors swung open, and the warmth in my chest turned to ice.

The receiving chamber statues were toppled and shattered. Cracks sundered the marble floor. Who could do this?

Who would *dare*? I drifted forward and winced at the sound of glass and stone crunching under my shoes.

"Amy?" My voice echoed into the quiet. The quiet was always thick here, like a living, breathing thing, but now I felt nothing in the silence—no life, just a hollow emptiness.

I strode on, paces lengthening, icy rage spreading in my veins. Every fallen column, every shattered dais—it would have taken an army to do this, or a god.

Where was Amy? She never would have let this stand.

I was running when I rounded a corner and slipped in a pool of blood. Bright red splashes had fanned up the marble walls and left dripping streams. Their source, the body of a young boy, ripped open from groin to gullet. It was so unexpected, so out of place, that for a few moments, I did nothing, just stared at the boy's glassy, unfocused eyes. I hadn't known him, but the same family had served these halls for as long as I could recall. I knew his blood, now painting the floor.

I knelt down and touched the boy's neck. No pulse—I hadn't expected one—but his skin was warm. Whoever had done this could still be here, carving through my home, violating the sanctity of the temple.

Magic broiled, seeping from the air and the ground. It gathered around me like a cloud of darkness. *My* home. *My* magic. Rage burned bitter and sharp at the back of my throat. Old words fell from my lips, and here, in the halls, they quickly stirred the power residing in my soul.

This attack would not go unpunished.

"The Soul Eater has returned." I stepped over the body, pulled the darkness around me, and headed deeper inside my home. "And I'm hungry."

CHAPTER 11

I heard them before seeing them—a storm of snarls, yips, and growls.

I'll devour them all.

The door to my mother's chambers flung open—untouched—in front of me. Jackals—countless numbers of them—tore muscle and flesh from my mother's bones. They bickered and snarled over her carcass, like she was meat.

The ice inside me shattered. A vicious, barbed spell built up in a blinding surge and exploded outward. With no focus, no anchor point, it whirled around the room, sweeping through the demons it touched, sinking its claws deep into their souls, and ripping them into shreds from the spirit outward. The spell swelled, and I fed, taking them all in, their poisonous darkness filling me up.

I fell hard to my knees as the screams poured in, on and on, threatening to sever my soul. Heavier and heavier, they pushed down. So many and so much darkness. I *could* contain them. I had to. None would escape.

I doubled over and heard the sound of my own ragged cry until it twisted into a monstrous roar. And then it was over.

Silence flooded the room, only interrupted by my tattered gasps.

The quiet was too thick, too heavy.

I smelled hot blood and ash, tasted the souls on my lips, and felt them burn deep inside.

Ammit was gone. If her soul had been here, I'd probably devoured it. I might never know, and it was too late to find out.

"*Daquir*," I muttered, releasing the spellword, and watched the dancing embers eat up the remains of the demons and the only god who'd ever cared enough to guide me. She'd been my protector in a world filled with monsters, and she had been the biggest, most terrifying monster of all. Someone had gotten to her, someone she hadn't seen coming.

Hours could have passed, or minutes, or no time at all. I knew I should move, that time would continue with or without me, but if I moved, I might break. That many souls... I'd taken them all. They strained and heaved and wrestled, but they were mine. Delight and ecstasy raced through my veins, lighting them on fire. I could do anything in that moment—raze buildings, move mountains, devour the sky—and I wanted to take it all and make it mine. I could. I dug my fingers into the marble floor. Cracks snapped outward, sounding like the gunfire from the mortal realm. New York. I had to go back. Chuck, Bast, even Shukra needed me.

Godkiller.

I pushed my body into motion, watching the shadows shudder in the corner of my eye. A broken laughter bubbled up my throat. I swallowed it down—for now.

With every step, flakes of ash stirred. Slowly, my thoughts pulled away from the stretching power and organized themselves around the present. The chamber was in chaos. Furniture was scattered and broken. Ammit had fought, but not as strongly as she could have. The jackals had come for her while she was weak and waiting to take her slumber.

I wandered through the room, absently righting furniture or kicking aside broken statue fragments.

"Soul Eater?" A serving boy stumbled inside the room. On seeing me, he froze.

"Inform Anubis that Ammit has been killed," I said, voice cutting.

The boy hesitated. He couldn't miss the ash, and being of Ammit's house, he'd know what I'd done. He'd feel the pulsing magic broiling around me and taste it on his tongue.

"S-sire?" he stammered.

Anubis wouldn't react well to the news. The boy was afraid, with good reason.

I picked up a small box from where it had fallen near her bed. Hieroglyphs of my mother's name ran along its edges, coupled with a symbol I didn't recognize—that of an animal with the body of a jackal and the head of a snake. Gems glittered at its corners. The artwork was precise, and old, before my time. The box was important. I knew every item of Ammit's, every hiding place, every sacred token, but not this.

I gave the lid a twist. It didn't move. I tried again, failing to crack the seal.

"Sire, I—"

I launched the box across the room. It bounced off the wall and skidded across the floor in front of the trembling kid.

"Go or by the damned I'll sunder your soul where you stand!" A compulsion whipped out with the words.

The boy's whole body jerked upright, out of his control, and then he was gone, sandals slapping on the hallway until the silence devoured that noise too.

I stared at the empty doorway and listened to the dark things inside me scream.

Whispers crept into the chamber. *Liar. Thief,* they hissed. Then I heard laughter, twisted and malicious. Madness. The laughter was mine.

Too many souls.

Too much darkness.

Too heavy.

I couldn't stay here in that room. If I did, I'd never leave. Already part of me wanted to stay and take up the mantle again. It was mine, wasn't it? I'd judge them all and find them damned.

Liar. Thief, the whispers proclaimed. They'd be silenced once I devoured them all.

The laughter cracked and fell away.

I placed one foot in front of the other. That was how all journeys started, no matter their destination. One step and then another. Simple, really. One step. Two. Three. Faster.

No, I couldn't stay. A world away, people needed me. But more than that, if I stayed, I'd fall, and this time, there would be nothing left of my soul worth saving.

I picked up the little box and left. I paid the ferryman with Osiris's final coin. He didn't speak, and neither did I.

The oars stroked through the river of souls, swift and silent.

⚬⚬⚬

By the time I returned to New York, another day had passed.

My apartment greeted me with its typical New York somber ambiance. Scaffolding had clad the building for weeks. Boards and poles blocked the light. Considering some of my more sensitive activities, I had kept the blinds closed. I stepped into the cold and the dark, not bothering with the lights.

"Poison" started playing from my cell the second I got in. I switched it off, found the vodka bottle and a glass, and slumped in the chair by the bed.

I'd witnessed horrors, I'd been on the receiving end, and I'd been the perpetrator. It took a lot to break me down. The last few days had ground all the fight right out of me—that and the slippery wave of souls rippling under my skin.

The sounds of traffic lulled my already numbed mind. The alcohol did the rest.

Maybe I should have stayed in the underworld. Anubis was difficult to speak with, but he might have known something. As it was, all I'd done was arrive too late to stop my mother's slaughter and run.

I swallowed a deep gulp of vodka.

I'd made a deal to kill Thoth, for nothing.

"Great job, Ace." I lifted the glass in salute. "This is why we don't work for gods." I took a drink, letting it burn all the way down to the heat inside my soul.

Give me stupid rich kids any day. They were so much easier to frighten.

I should have been trying to think around what was going on, but really, I couldn't think at all. Too many black souls whirled inside. I'd swallowed down a storm. I could probably threaten Osiris with all the juice I'd absorbed. I'd fail though. I always did.

A few knocks at my door punctured my thoughts. I waited, in the dark, in the quiet. Shu wouldn't knock. She would have kicked the door in. Whoever it was would go away.

"I know you're back."

Bast. I smiled a bitter, hollow smile, and rolled the cool glass against my cheek. She wouldn't leave. Gods didn't know when to quit.

"Come on in."

She clicked the door closed behind her and strode over, stopping a few feet away to cross her arms and frown at me. "Why are you wearing a suit? I thought it was all robes and jewelry back home?"

"There was a party. Didn't yah hear?" I slurred.

Her frown darkened. She snatched my bottle away. "This isn't like you."

"Clearly this is exactly like me. Who else would I be like? Give that back."

She looked at the bottle and then at me. "Your eyes are dark."

"Yes, they are, so give me the vodka back and leave me stewing in the souls of the damned."

"How many?"

"I lost count."

"Why?"

I finished off the vodka in my glass and leaned my forehead against it. "Ammit is dead. I got there too late. I...lashed out."

Between one long blink and the next, Bast disappeared, but I heard her rattling around my kitchen. When she returned, she poured me a fresh glass, filled hers, and then sat on the bed. Her knee brushed against mine. I expected her to flinch away, but she didn't. She had to feel the darkness I'd gorged on. How could she stand to look at me, to touch me?

"Anubis will be furious," she said, tasting her vodka and scowling into her glass.

"That's nothing new." I slumped lower in my chair and closed my eyes. "I'm tired."

She knew I didn't mean physically tired, but soul tired. It was a whole other exhaustion, an all-consuming tiredness that ate me up from the spirit out.

"You're too young to be tired. You're grieving."

"Grieving?" The insane laughter was back, but this time I

confined it to my thoughts. "She kicked me out, Bast. She gave me—my life, my soul, all of me—to Osiris to do with as he saw fit. She knew exactly what she was doing." Maybe she'd hated me all along—the liar, the soul thief. "There was no love lost between Ammit and I."

She stayed quiet, probably because she knew the truth: I'd deserved it.

"Don't do this to yourself."

"I'm not doing anything. It's everyone else screwing with me."

"You're not the same. I was wrong."

She hadn't seen the smile on my face when I'd consumed the soul of the demon that had attacked Chuck. She hadn't heard me laugh after I'd gorged myself on jackals. And she didn't know how I'd drunk the blood of an innocent with Osiris and Isis looking on. I hadn't changed. If anything, I was worse for pretending I could change. Osiris knew that and probably always had.

She settled her hand on my arm, drawing my eye. "I'm sorry about Ammit, I am, but I need you, and not like this."

What did she expect from me? I couldn't save people. That wasn't me. I condemned them.

She looked at me with hope, and that was even more crippling than if her dark eyes had accused me. I didn't deserve her hope.

She moved her hand away, but I caught it and turned it over, marveling at how smooth her touch was. She briefly looked into my eyes, despite knowing what resided there.

"Don't go." I hated how I sounded. I'd been the one to leave her, but I couldn't be alone. I didn't want to be tired and alone, listening to the whispers condemn and the souls accuse.

"Ace..."

Lifting her hand, I lightly kissed the backs of her fingers.

She would turn me away, and so she should. A muscle fluttered in her cheek, her teeth gritting. We were thinking the same thing, how this was a terrible idea.

I set my glass down on the side table and pushed from my chair. Slipping a hand into her hair, I kissed her before she could tell me to stop. A gentle taste—something to keep me from the dark. When she opened up to me, I welcomed her and deepened the kiss, caught by a raw and sudden urgency to lose myself in the feel of her.

Her fingers made quick work of my shirt buttons. Her bold hands pulled me closer. Her nails scraped my back, and then it all became a rush of hungry touches and breathless pleas. I'd missed her, more than I'd ever let on to anyone, including myself. I'd let her go and pushed her away because I'd seen her soul, and it was light. So light and so good. I hadn't expected that.

Light and dark. The dark in me would have destroyed the light in her.

But after all that had happened, I needed her with me. It was selfish, and I knew that too. I needed a little light before the dark swallowed me down for good.

I really hadn't changed at all.

CHAPTER 12

I came around slowly, aware of a curious weight settled across my chest. For a few blissful moments, all I knew was the sweet, wild scent of meadows and an exotic musk—Bast's scent. She smelled like far-off places, like forgotten memories, and my steady heartbeat quickened with keen and foolish hope. I could pretend, just for a few moments, that I deserved to be content. Then the sounds of New York filtered into my apartment and reality chased away my hiding place, reminding me I was the monster in this dream and that I didn't belong.

Bast ran a fingernail around my nipple and then sent those sharp nails lower. A scatter of delicious shivers stirred me fully awake. She hooked one leg possessively around mine and pulled herself over me. Her body was fluid in motion, muscles lean but firm—coiled strength—and her golden skin gleamed with the same luster as her alter ego's black coat. She prowled lower, trapping my thighs between hers. Where her warm skin brushed mine, shivers sparked. I'd lost myself in her smooth skin and maddening curves last night and wanted to again.

I reached for her face, hoping to draw her up into a kiss, but she batted my hand away and growled low in her throat. She tilted her head up, mischief glowing in her green cat eyes. She grinned, displaying sharp, pointed canines, and ran the tip of her tongue over her lip.

Last night was a blur. What had started as a questioning kiss had turned into ferocious need. The many scratches and bites throbbing on my shoulders and other parts were evidence of Bast's enthusiasm. We'd each taken what we needed from the other and hadn't been gentle about it. But now, with the look in her eyes and the feel of her tongue in its slow, deliberate exploration—there was more to this than quenching desires.

She pulled up, planted her hands on either side of my head, and locked her gaze inches from mine, pinning me beneath her. If I touched her, she'd slap my hand away again. That gaze was an order.

Prey, it said. *Don't move. You're mine.*

My quick breaths betrayed my building anticipation. In five hundred years, no woman had trapped me quite like she did. I loved that about her, loved how fearless and dominant she was, but her dominance wasn't stolen by force. She had earned her alpha status.

I spread my hand against her hip, needing to touch her. Her responding growl reverberated low and deadly, thrumming through me and sweetening my desire, while also pooling heat way down below. I could have ignored the warning, ridden my hands up her back, pulled her down, and taken her, but that wasn't the game she wanted to play.

Leaning into my shoulder, she braced herself on an elbow and shifted her free hand lower, swirling her fingers across my bare skin.

My thoughts had funneled down to one thing.

Lower, I silently begged and may even have said it out loud. Lower her hand went, gliding, swirling.

"Look at me," she purred.

I turned my head and locked gazes with her. Her green eyes shone, and inside, her brilliance stirred.

I blinked and tried to turn my face away, breaking contact, but her hand caught my jaw and pulled me back.

"Look at me," she said again, this time teasing a thread of compulsion through the words.

I felt the push and opened my mouth to warn her, but she planted a finger on my lips, sealing away the protest.

She was playing a dangerous game, one I couldn't resist. I flicked my eyes up and her glare captured mine while her hand closed around my cock. I arched into her grip. I'd never been very good at self-control. She laughed, a deep, salacious chuckle, and collecting the wetness, she moved her hand in a way that made me forget all the warnings I needed to tell her.

Our gazes entwined, my soul tugging at hers, sinking threads of darkness into her light. Her soul embraced it, welcoming me—the innocent always did—but no soul could withstand mine. As I sank into her, and her hand worked its rhythm, and the pleasure beat at my barriers, chilling stabs of fear plunged in. I wanted to go deeper and wallow in her brilliance, like maybe I could cleanse myself of the darkness if I drowned myself in her light. It felt like coming home, like I would always be safe, always be welcome, until the darkness in me rose up like a storm on the horizon. Pleasure wrenched the shreds of resistance away. Her eyes drew me in and led me on, and I stalked her soul. I could take her, make her mine, and swallow her down. Heated need beat in time with her hand, and the darkness surged, hungry and all-consuming.

With a cry, I tore my gaze away and squeezed my eyes closed, maybe I'd even told her to stop, but her lips were on mine, her tongue pushing in. Her hands were suddenly on my face, and she lowered herself onto me, capturing all of me.

"It's okay," she whispered against my mouth, hips rocking, her body driving me toward the edge. "It was always okay."

I still had hold of her light and pulled it tighter, higher, harder. Snapping my eyes open, I pulled her down, twisted, flipping her onto her back, and thrust deep. Her nails dug into my shoulders, and for a few blinding moments, I froze. She arched, her lips parted, breaths coming fast and ragged, and I was sure I'd never seen any woman more beautiful than her. Body and soul, I could have both. A cruel, dark voice urged me to drink her down while she writhed and screamed her pleasure. I could devour her soul and fuck her until there was nothing left to take.

Horror thrust brittle ice through my veins. I whipped my head to the side, shattering the deep hold I had on her. Her soul slipped out of my reach like cool sand through my fingers.

"Bast, by Sekhmet, I can't..."

She quivered beneath me, sank her claws into my shoulders, and then raked them down my back. Pain chased away the fear, and when she growled my name, I lost myself in her until she came with a shattering cry.

A wide, gratified smile tugged at her lips. She pulled me down, darted her tongue into my mouth, and nipped my lip. I responded, but the kiss was hollow.

"You can't," I whispered, words failing. "We can't..."

I pushed out of her arms and swung my legs over the edge of the bed, showing her my back. She had no idea how close I'd come to yanking all of the brilliance out of her.

"You can't tempt me like that." Tremors rolled through me and my heart pounded, heavy and loud. Magic buzzed beneath my skin. It had been close—too close. Hunger plucked at the threads of pleasure, wanting more. Even now I wanted to turn and feed.

"You're stronger than you think."

"You don't know me." She thought she did. That was the problem.

Her hand ran up my back and over my shoulder. "I know you well enough. You'd never hurt me."

She was wrong—so wrong. If she could see what I saw and knew the kind of darkness I was made of, she wouldn't be here. She certainly wouldn't have let me touch her. If she knew how close she'd come to being mine...

"You liked it," she purred, close to my ear. Her hair tickled my shoulder and my neck, and her soft lips followed.

Oh, I liked it. I liked it a lot. I liked the feel of all that goodness, all that light, and how I could crush it and devour it until there was nothing left. The fact she'd held my gaze, challenged me, and ridden my pleasure at the same time, I had no idea how I'd resisted, and that terrified me.

"You need to leave."

She pulled back and a cool draft trickled down my back in her absence. The bed rocked, and I listened to her snatch up her clothes.

A slither of sunlight had pierced the gloom. My gaze strayed to the dust motes drifting through the daylight's glare, and then my thoughts fell to the spirits of the under-world, my home, and the death I'd found there. The sunlight fizzled away, my imagination turning the dust to ash.

When I twisted to look at Bast, she was tugging on her waistcoat. She kept her eyes down and focused on the buckles. Her fingers trembled. I wanted to tell her I was sorry, that I hadn't meant for things to get so out of control, that she should never have come to me for help, and that this was a mistake—again.

Instead, I asked, "Why did you decide to have the child?"

Her head jerked up. "Because"—she flipped her short hair out of her eyes—"I wanted to show you that you're capable of more than darkness."

Her words struck me like a punch to the gut. I slumped forward and shuddered. She didn't know how bad it had gotten in the underworld. She didn't know the hundreds of innocents I'd devoured. She didn't know the high I craved when every soul went down.

And the girl, our daughter—the girl with no home and no hope. I prayed to whatever god would listen to me that she wasn't like me.

Capable of more than darkness. Emotion, sweeping and heady, caught a hold of me and I was glad Bast couldn't see my face. Why did her words hurt like this, like someone had punched into my chest and torn out my heart?

More than darkness. I wished it were true, and that was where the ache came from. I wanted her—the woman with the soul filled with hope and light—to be right, but she was so very wrong.

"You should look to Osiris for answers," Bast was saying.

I dragged my hand down my face and blinked my sight back into focus, back into the room and my life. When I turned again, my smile was back, plastered on my face like a mask.

"If I look to that bastard for anything, it'll be for a place to stab Alysdair in deep." I heard my voice going through the motions and saying the same things, but the hurt her words had caused rippled on.

Bast collected her coat and shrugged it over her shoulders. "Besides him and Anubis, there's nobody left who can control the jackals. Anubis hasn't been interested in any of us for as long as I can remember. But Osiris? There's something about him... Like he's buying time."

Osiris's words came back to me—how he'd been planning

for millennia and how time was something a god had a surplus of. Yes, it would be better to focus on Osiris and the murders and not on the fact that I'd almost killed a good woman because it *felt good* to fuck and devour at the same time. If she knew the truth, she'd know I wasn't fit to be a father, and she wouldn't hold out the foolish hope that I could change.

I fell back on the bed and propped my head up on my hand. "This—you and me—can't happen again."

Her lips turned down. She managed to mask the pain in her eyes, but only after I'd seen the glimmer. "Don't worry. There's no chance of that."

Apologies were back on my lips, but I swallowed it. This was for her own good, and telling her *sorry* would have been for mine.

"I need to go," she said but didn't move. Her gaze glided over me. All the desire was gone, and regret hooded her eyes. "You could stop feeling sorry for yourself and help me."

"Why would Osiris attack your blessed?" I asked, turning the topic away from me while neglecting to mention I'd made a deal to kill a god so I could return to the home I'd been cast out of for her blessed.

She sighed. "I don't know. I haven't spoken to Osiris in decades."

Interlocking my hands behind my head, I stared at the protection spellwork coating my ceiling, and traced the swirling lines and intricate hieroglyphs. The pattern helped clear my head and focus.

Bast noticed where my gaze was pinned. "Protection spells? You're paranoid."

"Ever have someone try to slit your throat in your sleep?"

Her brow shot up. "No."

Of course she wouldn't have. Everyone loved her. Which begged the question: Who would target her blessed women?

"There's a connection between the women," she said. "Something we're not seeing. I'll go over their activity for the last few months and see if I can find anywhere they converged."

A pounding on the door rattled my windows.

"Ace!" Shu barked from the landing.

Bast's lips twitched. She flicked her hair out of her collar and strode toward the door.

"Don't open—"

Shu entered my apartment like a whirlwind in a fur coat. She barely spared Bast a glance and didn't blink at me sprawled naked on the bed. "You have no idea the shit I've had to deal with in the last twenty-four hours, and here you are, fucking your ex?"

I didn't move. She wasn't pissed off that I was screwing Bast. She hadn't known whether I was back from the underworld or if I'd ever come back. Her anger buried what I knew had been real, heartfelt fear. Had I not come back, she would have had no choice but to return to the underworld, and the souls wouldn't be as welcoming to her as they had been with me.

"Bye, Ace." Bast sauntered out the door without a backward glance, leaving me to face Shu.

Five and a half feet of fierce ex-demon was fuming at the foot of my bed. "You turned off your cell."

I padded naked to the shower. My bare ass wouldn't deter her—very little did. Sure enough, she followed. I shut the shower door closed on her glower. "The kid?"

"Yes, the kid. He's not a kid anymore. If you had your cell on you'd know Cujo has a lead. You need to get down there and deal with it. He's been fielding reports to keep the cops from getting killed."

I'd never tell her, but she was exactly what I'd needed: a reason to throw on my coat, pick up Alysdair, and go to work

—a distraction. She kept my dark thoughts at bay. Ironic, considering who—what she was.

"Okay." I switched on the water and buried my face in the hot jets. Thoroughly soaked, I asked, "Shu, do you know any illusion spells?"

"What for?" she snapped loud enough for me to hear over the hissing water.

"Insurance."

A guttural sound filled the bathroom, the growl sounding more demon than human. "You need a lot of power to pull off one of those."

I could just make out her outline, rigid and stubborn, through the fogged glass. I waited, knowing she couldn't resist the promise of a challenging spell.

"I can craft one, but I can't activate it," she said. "Not in this useless body. But you could, in your current state."

"That's what I thought." I ran my hands through my hair, washing off the smells of sex, ash, and the underworld.

"What are you thinking?" she asked.

That the darkness in my soul will never wash off, I thought.

⚜

TRINITY CHURCH, ON BROADWAY, HAD ONCE BEEN THE focal point for the Lower Manhattan community and a beacon of hope for arriving ships. I remembered its destruction—twice. First by fire and then after a devastating snowstorm had weakened its walls beyond repair. New York's highrises had sprouted around its third incarnation, reducing the impressive church, with its piercing spire and gothic embellishments, to a toy among monoliths erected in honor of the modern world. Like the old gods, the church stood proud and defiant, but lost in the shadows of the new world.

By the time I bumped the Ducati onto the curb, the weak

winter sun was setting, but clung on to neighboring Wall Street and pseudo-darkness had descended on the church grounds. I left the bike on the sidewalk, risking a ticket. It was a whole lot easier chasing down a demon using 205-horse-power than by foot.

Alysdair was snug against my spine. The coat hid her profile, but not the handle and hilt. I usually confined the sword to nighttime use, but after the events of the last few days, having Alysdair within reach gave me options I sorely needed.

Collar up, I ducked through the high construction fencing and out of sight of passersby.

The church was in the throes of a substantial renovation project. The demon had likely sensed something of the old powers in the church grounds. Construction workers had reported strange noises and a sighting of what they'd described as a rabid homeless man to the cops. Cujo had fielded the reports and passed them on to me.

I'd been inside a handful of times in the past, most recently during 9/11. The inside of the church was a resplendent sight when properly illuminated. But today, with the aid of a few work lights, all that loomed out of the gloom were rows of sheet-covered pews.

I hesitated at the main aisle, motionless, and listening. New York buzzed and snarled outside. I listened deeper, to the quiet inside the church and how it soaked up the noise. And there, at the back of the church in the darkest part, deep breathing rumbled.

"Remember me?" I asked, not needing to raise my voice for the quiet to carry it. "You're a long way from home."

"So...are...you."

From the grainy growls behind those words, I was betting there wasn't anything left of Jason Montgomery.

Alysdair whispered free of her sheath. Her weight and

balance felt good and right in my hands. No more consuming souls. This demon was going out by Alysdair's grace, not mine.

"There's only one way this goes down."

"Soul Eater. Liar...thief." Its hisses sailed down the aisle and sounded exactly like the whispers back home.

"I'm all those things," I replied with a knowing smirk. "And more."

And you should be afraid.

Alysdair's pale green glow washed over the pews a few steps ahead, lighting the way.

A large shape shifted in the darkness behind the altar. Roughly the size of a man, it could have been mistaken for someone hiding under blankets, but those leathery sheets weren't blankets.

A quick spot check for exits confirmed the only way out was behind me. When it sprang, and it would, I'd be faster. Gripping Alysdair in my right hand, I raised the sword in a reverse grip, and fixed the mound in my sights. A few more steps and I could skewer it to the wall, ending this before it began.

Then the words started. Spellwords, from a demon? Ballsy.

"Oh no you don't." I lunged.

The demon flung its massive bat-like wings open, knocking Alysdair clean out of my hands, and punched me in the chest. I flew back, slammed into a pew, and fell forward. Damn, those wings had reach. With an ear-splitting screech and a blast of air, the demon beat its wings and rose above the altar in ungainly, inexperienced jerks. Its twisted gargoyle face rippled with rage. Hollow eye sockets glowed red. Jason Montgomery was long gone.

I spared a quick glance for Alysdair but couldn't find her. So much for abstaining from soul eating. That promise had lasted a pathetic few hours. Spitting a curse, I pushed to my feet.

The demon screamed triumphantly and swiveled its glowing eyes onto me.

I smiled. "Hungry? I know I am."

"POLICE! Get your hands up!"

I snarled as all my plans shattered. Life had been so much easier when people ran away from demons. Now, too many of them rushed in. I lifted my hands so the cops could see I wasn't a threat—at least not to them.

Flashlight beams flicked over the pews, down the aisles, up the wall, and landed on the demon hovering in the air and whipping up a dust storm.

"DON'T MOVE!" More shouts. Boots scuffing. Gear rattling. They'd get themselves killed within seconds. Opening fire on the demon wouldn't stop it, but it would give it a target. Those talons would slice through the cops and their Kevlar like they were made of paper.

I thrust out my left hand. "*Hurzd.*"

Power throbbed through me, heady and intoxicating. The demon's flaming eyes widened, its wings locked up, and the thing tumbled out of the air, thumped onto the altar, and slid off.

"Sorry, peaches, no time for foreplay."

"DON'T MOVE!"

I sprang forward and clasped my hands on either side of the demon's hideously deformed face. The spell tumbled forth, words binding together and digging deep, and into the slippery darkness I went. Even as boots thudded up the aisle and the cops shouted at me to step away from the *thing*, the spell latched on and yanked.

Power—dark and delicious—buzzed. The laughter returned, and I was right at home. Arms hooked around mine and tugged me off the demon. I felt it distantly and heard the cops barking orders as though they were in another room. I was thrown facedown and someone dug a knee into my back, wrenched my arms behind me, and slapped on the cuffs.

"... used against you in a court of law. You have a right to an attorney. If you cannot afford an attorney, one will be appointed for you."

Laughing probably didn't help, but there it was, bubbling from my lips.

"*Daquir*," I whispered.

Sprites of fire danced over the demon's carcass, startling the cops who aimed their weapons at the rapidly vanishing remains, for all the good it would do them. Activity buzzed. Radios crackled. And in seconds, the demon was gone, turned to ash.

The cops muttered among themselves, no longer sure what they'd witnessed, and looked at me like I might sprout wings. They had no idea I was the real stuff of nightmares. In a few hours, they'd convince themselves it couldn't possibly be a demon they'd seen. It was a trick of the light. Fearful minds concoct imaginary foes.

After they bundled me into the back of a squad car, I dropped my head back and closed my eyes. "I get a phone call, right?"

"Back at the precinct," my police escort said from the cruiser's front seat and then asked, "What was that back there?"

"What was what?"

"The thing. I saw it."

"I didn't see anything." My smile was back, broader than ever.

CHAPTER 13

I got my phone call and my own holding cell. I was under arrest for a slew of minor offences. They had yet to connect me with the three dead kids from the midtown high-rise, and if my phone call paid off, they wouldn't get a chance. But if they found Alysdair, it wouldn't be too much of a stretch to place me on the roof where the kids had been butchered.

If my call didn't pay off, it might be time to leave the city. The thought of leaving New York wasn't pleasant. After a few decades, the city, its endless activity, its hard outlook, and its no-bullshit people were a part of me. I'd made a home here, settled here longer than anywhere else. But perhaps it was time. Stay in one place too long and the roots rot, so the old world saying goes.

It had been so much easier to slide under the radar when people weren't armed with cell phones and cameras. Now everything was filmed, recorded, and ferreted away into data-centers. It *was* more difficult than ever to hide—unless you happened to be like Osiris and relished hiding in plain sight.

A uniformed cop collected me from my cell and escorted me to an interrogation room.

The door clicked closed behind me, leaving me standing under the cool scrutiny of the straight-faced, charcoal-suited Thoth.

He appraised me from his sitting position at the table and said in a tone so flat and sharp it could have cut diamonds, "No cell can hold you."

I shrugged, finding myself restless under his gaze. He didn't exude power the same way Osiris did. Thoth's lurked deep. "I have to live this life. I'd prefer not to live it on the run."

He opened his briefcase, removed a slip of paper, and slid it across the table toward me. "The evidence is circumstantial. They have nothing to hold you. You'll be released. Sign here."

Hands still cuffed, I eyed the mirrored wall. Attorney-client conversations were confidential, but it wasn't the cops I was concerned about. Gods had many ways of eavesdropping on the unsuspecting.

After signing Thoth's form—as confident as I could be that the God of Law wasn't about to screw me over—I pushed the paper back across the table.

He gathered the document and neatly inserted it into the proper place inside his briefcase. Then he nudged one of his pens back in line, making it parallel with its neighbor. Gods forbid anything was out of place. He'd have a fit if he saw my filing system.

"You can't afford me, Mister Dante," Thoth said, still cold, still flat. He had about as much spark in him as a reanimated corpse.

"No, I can't afford you, but like I said, I have information to trade." What I was about to do, if it went wrong, could start a feud that would have far-reaching consequences. Or

Thoth might try and kill me where I stood, because that would certainly be one fine way out of this mess.

Thoth leaned both elbows on the table and steepled his fingers. With his back straight, his shoulders rigid, and the dash of a goatee narrowing his already thin face, he reminded me of a blade, the kind of blade forged to look plain but that could slice through anything in its path. No doubt about it, my next words would either free me or condemn me.

He waited, probably wondering if he could trust a word I said. *Liar. Thief,* he'd be thinking.

"Osiris suspects you're screwing his wife," I said. The ground didn't tremble. Thunder didn't crack. Maybe I'd get away with this.

Thoth blinked twice and lifted his chin. "That's unfortunate and quite incorrect."

"Of course." I couldn't tell from his blank expression whether he was lying. I couldn't read a damn thing on his face. I'd just told him the most powerful god, outside of the elusive Amun-Ra, believed he was screwing his wife, and Thoth had barely flinched. He really was hardcore. "But you are meeting with her?"

He blinked quickly again and abruptly stood. "That I cannot confirm or deny."

You just did, I thought.

Thoth straightened his cuffs and sleeves so they perfectly lined up.

"Let me be clear, Mister Dante." He looked up, and something dangerous peered out from behind his slate-gray eyes. "Isis's love for her husband is enduring and eternal. It is the one constant in our ever-changing lives, much like the air we breathe or the ground we walk upon. There is no god, no force in this realm, the underworld, or the afterlife, that can sever their bond."

"Besides themselves?"

He briefly bowed his head, conceding. Either he didn't know Osiris like I did, or he didn't care that the god had his crosshairs lined up on his back. And I was the unfortunate one who'd have to pull the trigger. But I had room to maneuver. I'd agreed to kill Thoth; I hadn't agreed not to warn him first.

"Armies have marched off the back of love," I said. "Thousands of people die every day for it."

"Love is indeed a potent motivator."

Thoth and Isis weren't screwing, I knew that much, but they were meeting in secret, and that alone would be enough to put a wedge between Osiris and his wife.

"Whatever is going on between you and Isis, unless you tell Osiris the truth, it will get you killed." Killing a god was no idle threat, and I'd just laid it out bare.

Thoth's faultless expression gained a few fracture lines around the mouth. It was probably the closest he came to grimacing. "I cannot."

"His suspicions will consume him." *And the rest of us,* I added silently.

Thoth's bloodless lips pulled into a reed-thin smile. *By the gods, he does smile!* And it was a horrible thing to witness. "I appreciate the concern, but it's not necessary."

"Oh, I'm not concerned for you."

Thoth stood, picked up his case, and came around the table. Easily a foot taller than me, he peered down his narrow nose, meeting my eyes for as long as he dared before shifting the briefcase to his left hand and straightening his tie. "We are each confined to our word."

"Indeed we are."

He knew I'd be coming for him and that I'd told him more than enough to protect himself—and hopefully me—when the time came.

"I'm sure we'll meet again soon, Mister Dante."

"Of that, I have no doubt."

Without delay, he marched out of the interrogation room. The cop entered moments later. She unlocked my cuffs and spared me a smile. "That's one efficient attorney you have there, Mister Dante. You're free to collect your personal belongings and go."

I rubbed my sore wrists and wondered if I'd earned myself a friend in Thoth, or an enemy.

SHUKRA WAS WAITING OUTSIDE THE PRECINCT, HER FACE like thunder. A pair of sunglasses hid her eyes and protected them from the glare coming off the fresh snow dump. The rest of her, wrapped in a fur-lined coat, stood rod straight and immobile, warning me she was about to grill me.

"What part of *don't get caught* did you not understand?"

I flicked my coat collar up and flashed her a smile. "Like a red rag to a bull."

"I hate you."

"I noticed."

"How did you get off?"

"Thoth."

She balked at that, probably wondering where I'd gotten the cash to hire one of the best attorneys in the city. Her questions were incoming and would hit once she worked through the details in that steel-trap mind of hers.

Plucking my cell from the police-issued plastic bag, I switched it on and waited for it to boot up. My breath misted the air. Steam rolled off the street and the cold gnawed on my face and fingers. Squinting into the too-bright winter sun, I spotted a red Ducati parked outside the precinct's parking lot.

Shu shook her head. "Wasn't me, but I did pick up Alysdair from the church. It tried to eat me. You're welcome."

I headed for my bike and resisted the sudden and alarming urge to thank Shu. Her touching the sword was no minor thing. The blade had likely burned her and tried to draw her soul into itself. Her going within three feet of the blade was an unexpected act of kindness from a demon that supposedly wanted to scoop out my insides with a spoon. She'd want compensation.

The Ducati's keys were waiting in the ignition. Thoth *was* thorough. It would be a shame when I had to kill him.

"Was the Montgomery problem dealt with?" Shu asked, stamping her feet and puffing into her hands.

"Yeah." My cell chimed a message alert. "But I've collected a few more since then."

I didn't have to tell Shu anything, but we'd learned over the years that secrets didn't last long and usually caused more trouble than they were worth. Besides, she knew my soul. There was no greater secret than that. Bizarrely, I knew I could trust her. Besides Osiris and Cujo, she was the only other being who knew the exact details of my curse—because it was also hers. In five centuries, she'd never told another soul.

My cell vibrated. I glanced at the screen. *VOICE MESSAGE: BAST.*

"We need to talk," I told Shu and lifted the cell to my ear.

"Ace, two more of my blessed are dead. I'm on my way to a suspected third. Call me back."

The message ended, and another began, this one from a few hours ago. *"Chuck is missing. I think I've found their connection. Meet me at the corner of two-thirtieth and Edgewood. The others are dead, Ace. All of them."* The message ended, cutting to silence.

"Damnit." I dialed Bast's number, but the call rang out. "Shu, are you armed?"

"Always."

I swung my leg over the bike and rocked it upright. "Follow me. Keep up."

Almost three hours had passed since that call, and Bast hadn't called back. Whichever way I looked at it, my ex-wife's silence was a bad omen.

The Ducati roared to life beneath me. I rolled the bike onto the road, spotted Shu climbing into her beat-up two-seater sports car, and opened the bike's throttle. The tires gripped with a screech, launching me through blurry New York streets. Shu wouldn't keep up, but she'd find me. She always did.

Chuck was missing. Bast's women were dead. My mother had been slaughtered in her own chamber. The jackals suggested the events were linked. It was unlikely that Ammit had been pregnant like the other victims. Perhaps she'd known something, and the killer—with enough clout to turn the Devourer's jackals against her—had wanted her silenced. As much as the thought sickened me, I had to talk with Osiris.

I turned the bike onto Edgewood and rolled to a halt. EMTs, cop cars, and a growing crowd blocked the residential street. Was Bast here? I tried her cell again. Nothing.

The crowd strained against a stretch of police tape. I carved my way through them to the front. The stark winter sun highlighted bright splashes of blood in the snow. Bulky body bags gave the rest of the scene its finality. Someone or something had ripped through a squat, single-story building and torn through anyone who had gotten in its way.

Radio chatter drew my eye to an animal control van. Bast?

Among the slushy mess of blood and snow near the front

steps, I spotted large paw prints. Bast wouldn't have done this, but she'd been here.

"Ace." Shu drew me away from the frontline, thumbs tapping on her phone. "This address is listed as a modeling agency, but there are some indications online that that wasn't all they did."

"Like what?" I scanned the crowd, the cops, and the dozens of vehicles, but Bast wasn't here. She could have picked up the killer's scent and started tracking them while I played catch-up. Why hadn't she called me?

"Escorts."

I spotted an ambulance with its rear doors hanging open and started toward it. "Escorts as in professional friends or escorts with benefits?"

"The benefits kind," Shu replied.

Escorts—the connection Bast had mentioned. The dead women had been on the payroll?

An EMT loitered near the back of the ambulance with her head down, busy filling out paperwork.

"Shu, go over there, be dramatic, and make it good. I need a few minutes alone with the witness in the back of that ambulance."

Her sunglasses couldn't hide the way her eyes lit up at the promise of mayhem.

"Don't hurt anyone," I quickly added before she could summon a biblical plague.

"Happy to help." She tucked her phone away, removed her sunglasses, and sauntered toward the EMT.

I took up a hapless bystander position at the front of the ambulance, checked that the driver was busy in the cab, and waited for Shu's signal. Sure enough, she let out a cry and dramatically fell into the crowd, causing enough of a ruckus for the EMT to rush in.

I climbed into the back of the ambulance, spooking the guy wrapped tightly in a space blanket. He shrank away.

"Hey, just a few questions—not gonna hurt you."

"Who are you?" He had the wide, glassy-eyed look of someone in shock, and he blinked at me like I might be a figment of his imagination.

"Someone who can help." Shu's commotion continued outside, but I didn't have long before the EMT returned. No time for small talk. "Did you see who did this?"

He shook his head. "No, man, I was out back. We heard the shouts, and then the screams started...I heard Jimmy sayin'..." He trailed off, the memories dragging him under. He'd be reliving them for a while.

He swallowed and looked down at his hands cradled in his lap. "He was begging, yah know? You're supposed to stay in your room. They told us on that terrorist training course, yah know, after nine-eleven. If anything happens, like this... I mean, not like this. Nobody expects someone to come in and start...cutting."

"Just one person?"

He nodded. "I think so. The door was shut, but I heard..."

"Did anyone say anything that could help? Any names? Anything at all?"

"Jimmy..." He winced. "He said the girl wasn't here."

"What girl?"

"I could hear Jim clearly, but..." When he looked at me, there were questions in his expression, and confusion clouded his eyes. "I should remember, shouldn't I? Something? Anything? The cops asked. They looked at me like... I dunno. I should—I can't..."

"What girl?" I pressed, keeping my voice calm while my heart raced.

"I don't know, man." His fingers were trembling so he curled them into fists. "Jimmy said she was in the old warehouse apartments down by pier fifteen and then...and then he didn't say anything else. I found him." His shoulders shook. "His throat was..."

I had a lead. It was something. "Thank you."

"Shock, right? Why I can't remember? It's shock. I mean, the cops said it was. It makes you forget. Makes you see things?" He giggled in a wholly unhealthy way. "Because, man, when I saw that panther, I thought I'd lost my shit for good."

I smiled in what I hoped was a reassuring way. "You've been very helpful."

He smiled back and puffed out a small laugh. "I wish there was more I could tell yah."

I turned to jump down from the ambulance but paused. "Did the panther happen to say anything?"

He frowned, and his eyes cleared. "Cats don't talk, dude."

"Of course." It had been worth a shot.

I jumped down from the ambulance and strolled back to my bike, keeping my head down and collar up. I knew the address he'd mentioned, pier fifteen. The converted ironwork factory had once housed low-income families. Now it was marked for demolition to make way for a new waterside "village." Pier fifteen was the regular site of muggings, shootings, and all the other wonderful crimes that seeped into areas that had been cut out of New York and left to rot.

Shu was waiting beside my bike, shades back on, and lips pressed into a grim line.

"The witness was suffering from memory lapses," I said. "His pupils were dilated and he was exhibiting slight delirium. Symptoms of shock."

"Godstruck," she replied, echoing my thoughts exactly. "You think this is *Osiris's* doing?" She hissed out his name like the taste of it burned her tongue.

"I think it's a possibility and one we need to consider before we go any further. The attack here, it was different. I saw paw prints large enough to be Bast's, but no sign of the jackals. The jackals are search and destroy. This was...this was someone who's run out of patience."

"I'll get Alysdair." Shu marched away and disappeared around the street corner.

She wouldn't like what I was about to tell her. If this was Osiris's doing, she couldn't get involved, and there was nothing Shu hated more (besides me) than being sidelined.

I started the bike, rode around to where she'd parked her car, and pulled up beside her. She was leaning against the hood. I cut the engine.

"We can't stop him," she said, her sunglasses hiding her eyes.

I planted my feet on either side of the bike and straightened. "*We* can't."

Her cheek twitched. "I'm not sitting this out."

She wanted to bloody her daggers with Osiris's insides as much as I did. "There's no point in him making us both dance. If he gets us together, he'll screw with us, like always."

We shared the same memories of past *performances*, courtesy of Osiris. I'd turned to Vodka after the last time. Shu had other means of forgetting, but what they were she hadn't shared with me.

The growl that sounded in her throat was a sound not belonging to this world. Something of the Shukra from old lurked in that threat. "There's nothing left to hurt us with."

She was so sure of that. I wasn't. "Keep your cell on and go to my apartment. As long as we're apart, Osiris can't screw our souls down even harder than he already has."

"I'd like to see him try." That was a lie driven by fear. She wouldn't and neither would I. Being shackled to the soul of your worst enemy was just one of the many painful and inventive methods Osiris used as torture. He'd had a few millennia to think up new and exciting ways of doing far worse. "I'll claw out his eyes and feed them to his bitch wife."

She may have once been powerful enough to do it too. Before the curse, before Osiris had dragged her into my punishment.

"If this is Osiris, I'll deal with it," I said. "We can't be together around him. It has to stay that way."

"Fine, but next time, I go alone and stick my daggers in him."

If only it were that simple. "I tried that, remember?"

She looked away, sending her gaze down the street. She was the first to find me after Isis had finished punishing me for my assassination attempt on her husband. In every image and statue, Osiris was depicted as holding a flail for a reason.

"I don't like this," she said, her words no less angry because of their calm undertone. "I don't like not knowing. I don't like being put on the bench. I don't like you." She reached in through the open car window, retrieved Alysdair from inside, and with a snarl, threw the sword at me.

I snatched it out of the air before the weighty sword could smack me in the face.

Her top lip rippled. "And I don't like that damn sword."

"Noted." I pushed Alysdair home inside its sheath. Shrugging the substantial weight into place against my back, I felt lighter for having the sword where it belonged.

"Don't get dead," Shu grunted and climbed into her car.

I started the bike and launched away from Shu. She wouldn't follow. In everything else, I had no sway over her. She'd fight, argue, and go against my wishes every step of the way, but when it came to Osiris, she heeded me.

CHAPTER 14

The quiet was back, as thick as soup, as heavy as the night that had fallen, and entirely unnatural. I rocked my bike onto its stand and peered through the fence at the converted apartment block. Across the ink-black river behind me, New York buzzed. A helicopter beat the air somewhere, horns blared, and sirens wailed. But ahead, silence devoured the sound as greedily as I devoured souls.

My darkness-adjusted eyes picked out a few glowing windows in the abandoned building. Up on the fifth floor, where scaffolding hugged the façade, someone was home.

I trudged across a churned-up wasteland of mud and grass and up the nearest stairwell. The apartments had been gutted months ago, most now open to the elements. Any signs of their former owners were long gone or buried under weeds.

Orange lantern light illuminated the first den and a few nervous eyes peered out of the gloom. My heart constricted when I thought of Chuck living like this, huddled in the dark alone. I moved on, purposely making my steps heavy and my presence known.

A few dens in, I found the first body. Fresh blood had crept from the corpse and shone like oil in the dark. Careful to keep one eye on the shadows surrounding me, I crouched down and pushed the body over: male, late forties, and his throat had been cut. His arms and hands were cut up too—defensive wounds.

The hairs on the back of my neck stirred. Something was watching me. Not a god—but someone with magic at their disposal.

Hands out, showing I was unarmed, I straightened and slowly turned.

The girl stood with her back to a window. Milky moonlight washed in from between the broken pane, casting her in silhouette. Her features were difficult to make out, but her eyes weren't. They captured every tiny sliver of light and sparked alive. I felt it then, the tug, the trap I could fall into. My soul hungered for hers, and hers hungry for mine.

She looked away at the same time I did.

"There are more bodies down the hall," Chuck said.

Bast had said Chuck was frightened, but if Chuck was afraid now, she hid all signs of it. She stood in the moonlight as rigid and cool as stone.

"I want to help you," I said.

"Help me?" Her teeth flashed in what could have been a smile or a sneer. "No one can help me."

"Who did this?"

I heard her swallow. "They came for me, the dogs, and then...someone did this, but I can't... I can't remember. I hid...and then here *you* are."

I deserved her mistrust. I wouldn't trust me either. "You don't have any reason to believe anything I say, but I'm the best chance you have at staying alive."

"You and that woman. You know what's going on, don't you?" With her chilling tone and her still body, I couldn't tell if she was angry, about to run, or too terrified to move. "You know everything?" she asked.

Bast would bring a whole world of pain down on me if she found out I'd told Chuck anything without her. I could lie, but something told me Chuck wouldn't fall for any more bullshit.

"Tell me the truth, and I'll go with you."

The truth? That Egyptian gods were real, most of them walked among normal people, and she was potentially one of them? The chances of that conversation going well were slim.

"I will, I'll tell you everything, but not here." I moved forward, just a step.

She backed up toward the window, hands spread and ready to lash out. Light fell across her face, washing all color from her skin. The glimmer in her eyes brightened. She looked too young to be here and to have death stalking her.

"I won't hurt you," I said.

"It's not you. It's me. What if...what if I did that?" Her last words came out in a whisper, and I understood what she was really afraid of. Not the jackals, not the unknown chasing her down, and not me. She was afraid of herself.

"You didn't kill him."

"I might h-have." She took another step back. "I... I do things. I *see* things."

"I know." I held out my hand, reaching for her. "Please, come with me."

She looked at my hand, at my face, and then finally at my eyes. If she looked deep enough, she'd see what I was truly made of, or maybe she'd see the fear—a fear just like hers.

Her face betrayed her emotions and thoughts so openly. First I saw confusion, and then I watched as she recognized that maybe she was looking into a distorted mirror and seeing more than just a man. Her eyes widened. Maybe she knew me. Maybe she'd always known me.

A jackal shot out of the darkness and slammed into her chest, throwing her off her feet and into the windowpane. Glass shattered. Chuck cried out. I grabbed for her ankle, but I was a second too late. Chuck and the jackal tumbled out the window.

I vaulted over the sill, expecting to fall several stories fast, but I abruptly landed on the scaffolding. Boards swayed under my feet. I grabbed the top rail to steady myself, but it snapped under my grip and fell into the darkness below. A few seconds later, the pole clanged against the ground. The wind howled and moaned, rocking the platform.

"Ace!"

Chuck was running down the boards, the jackal snapping at her heels. I bolted after them. Something vital twanged inside the framework, and the scaffold frame shuddered. Chuck slipped and went down. She reached to grab a hold of a rail. The sounds of boards cracking ricocheted into the night, and the board beneath her gave way.

She jumped—pale arms out—the jackal disappeared, and then something like a sledgehammer hit me in the shoulder. My breath whipped out of me, my hip hit a rail, and the weight of the thing almost shoved me over.

Teeth clamped into my upper arm and pain burst up my shoulder. Then the top rail I'd been pinned against snapped.

Air.

Weightlessness.

My heart lodged in my throat.

And then an abrupt tug yanked on my side, halting my fall. Ripping snarls rumbled around me—snarls from the jackal clamped on my arm and from where my coat had snagged on a rusted pole.

"Ace! Help!" The wind tossed Chuck's screams at me.

If she could shout, she was fine, unlike me, dangling over what was a fast fall to a painful impact.

The jackal growled and gurgled around the muscles in my shoulder, its teeth sinking deeper with every tug. Pain and anger bloomed, smothering any cohesive thought.

I reached around my front and clamped my hand around the jackal's muzzle. It snarled a warning. I dug my fingers into its mouth, sinking them around its sharp teeth, and heaved its jaw open. More snarls. The beast bucked, kicking its back legs against mine, apparently intent on making us both plummet several floors. It would tear my arm off at any second. Prying its jaws wasn't working. The jackal's eyes glowed, and deep inside, it was laughing.

My coat seams ripped, dropping me an inch. "Screw this."

"Ace!"

"Busy!" I curled my hand into a fist and punched the jackal in the jaw, once, twice, and then something cracked— its teeth or my knuckles. Again, I punched, giving it all I had and finally its grip released me. This time, when I got my hand around its muzzle, I yanked its jaw wide and kicked the jackal into the dark. A few seconds later, it landed with a heavy *thwump* below.

The scaffolding shuddered, and somewhere inside the structure, something else twanged. *This is a bad place to be.*

Hooking my good right arm around the lower guardrail, I heaved myself onto the boards in time to see the dark warehouse windows spewing packs of jackals onto the scaffolding, one after another, more and more. Some split my way, and others ran for Chuck.

"Sekhmet's ass." My left arm was damn near useless, and somewhere distantly, between the throbbing and the agony, my body was telling to go lay down.

Leave the girl, my doubts said. If she survived this, she'd be hunted to the ends of the earth. What was the point?

Chuck had crawled onto a lone scaffolding tower. The structure swayed away from the wall, tugged by the wind.

PIPPA DACOSTA

The jackals dashed right for her, and they'd clear the gap. The weight of one would be enough to topple the whole tower, and Chuck had five incoming.

None of this is her fault, I growled at that doubting voice inside my head.

"The window," I yelled, but the wind tore my shout away.

The window was her only escape, but she only had eyes for the jackals.

The first wave of jackals bore down on me, eyes ablaze, paws beating the boards, and claws scraping. I braced myself, brought my right shoulder down, and dug in when the first jackal hit hard. Using its own momentum, I shoved it upward and threw it over my back, hoping the damn thing would fall off the scaffold.

As I rose, I clamped my hand around Alysdair and swung the sword free, bringing it down in an arc and cutting through the flank of another jackal just as the demon sprang for the kill. They kept coming, and I kept slicing and slashing, Alysdair seeking flesh. The blade sang, aglow and hungry.

Chuck's scream pierced the howling wind. I lifted my head in time to see the scaffold lean out too far. She scrabbled to the higher side, balancing her weight against the fall, and then the first jackal leaped. It landed half dangling off the side. She kicked it in the jaw again and again, but the added weight was already pushing the scaffolding over.

She couldn't die. Not here and not like this. She'd survived on her own against everything out to get her. This wasn't how it ended for her. She deserved more.

I flung out my numb left hand, clenched my teeth against the agony burning up my shoulder, and spat the word, *"Hurzd!"*

Magic snapped out of me and hooked into the tower. The scaffold snagged in the air, mid-fall. A power ricochet slammed into me, snapping the magic taut, threatening to break my hold.

Chuck kicked at the jackal again, but the other demons were almost on her. She didn't see the next one coming until it skidded across the boards in front of her.

"The window!" I yelled.

Magic throbbed, and with every beat, it fed off my soul, and the blinding pain started gnawing on my strength.

Hold, damn it. Hold just a little longer. The tower jolted, but I had it. *A few more seconds.*

"The window, Chuck! I can't hold it."

I don't know if she heard me. I couldn't look, couldn't think of anything but holding the frame frozen in the air. The magic pulsed harder, over and over, draining me with every wave.

A jackal slammed into my back, throwing me off my feet. My cheek hit the wall, then the boards, and the world ripped and shattered. The spell snapped and lashed back, slicing soul deep. A cry shot from my throat, and in its wake, I heard the chiming clangs of Chuck's tower collapsing.

Capable of more than darkness, Bast's words mocked.

A jackal landed on my back. I got my hands under me and pushed up, but hot pain flared brightly in my shoulder, almost robbing me of the dregs of the strength I had left. Alysdair strummed in my hand. I gripped the sword tighter, listening to her sing.

The jackal's low growl trembled through my back. Its hot, stinking breath pushed against my neck. Drool slid down my cheek.

A high-pitched whistle sounded, and the jackal's weight lifted.

"Hey!" Chuck called.

The weight vanished.

I twisted and saw Chuck at the other end of the platform,

crouched low. Her golden eyes shone in the darkness, undeniable and hungry. The jackal started toward her, but didn't sprint like it had before. It managed a nervous trot and then sank onto its belly. Chuck stood, and with a stride too confident, she closed the distance between them. Those golden eyes glowed. Shit, she had the demon enthralled.

She stopped and looked the beast in its eyes.

Through the haze of pain and exhaustion, I finally realized what she was doing. "Don't," I growled. "Don't!"

Her eyes brightened. She drew back her lips in a smile I'd seen too many times in the mirror.

I got my feet under me, dragged Alysdair at my side, and staggered. I might be too late, like I'd been too late for everything, but I wouldn't let her damage her soul over this pathetic demon.

I plunged Alysdair into the beast's side, owning its death. *"Tra k-dae amcru-kak sra ksork, kosec amcru-kak esk kassrakamsk, omd kae kuir amcru-kak aeuirk."*

Chuck gasped and fell back, her connection with the demon severed. Her glittering, envy-filled eyes fell to Alysdair, the steel aglow.

When the soul was gone, I said, *"Daquir."*

The carcass fizzled to ash and embers. The others, sensing a Soul Eater among them, had vanished.

Chuck lifted her chin. Her bottom lip trembled and her skinny shoulders shook, but a new fierceness burned in her Soul Eater's eyes.

I had a lot of explaining to do.

CHAPTER 15

Chuck stepped into my dark apartment and stopped dead. Yellow eyes shone in the gloom.

I flicked on the lights. "Hey, Shu."

My business partner was sitting poised in the chair by my desk, giving her a direct line of sight to the door. She still wore her sophisticated pantsuit, but her demeanor was of a coiled snake about to strike, until she saw Chuck and the flicker of rage fizzled to curiosity.

"Bit young for your tastes, Acehole?"

The throbbing pain in my shoulder and the battering my body had taken had drained the fight right out of me. "Chuck, meet Shukra. Shu, meet Chuck."

Chuck stood rigid and was probably considering running. She'd likely sensed something was off about Shu, but given she had no idea what the hell was going on, she couldn't know Shu had once been a demon.

Shu pushed out of the chair and blatantly dragged her gaze over Chuck from head to toe and back again. "There's something familiar about you."

"Leave it," I warned, pushing the smallest hint of a compulsion into the words so she'd know to back off.

Her dark eyes caught mine. She didn't ask, but she did circle around Chuck in a way normal people didn't do unless they were psychopaths.

Chuck narrowed her eyes on the woman eyeing her up. "I thought I had issues."

I peeled my coat off my mangled shoulder. The fabric tugged on scabs of dried blood, reopening the wounds. Dumping the coat on the bed, I asked Chuck, "You hurt?"

"No," Chuck replied, and then added softly, "Don't think so."

Besides a few scrapes and bruises, she'd survived the warehouse relatively unscathed. I, on the other hand, hadn't. My coat was torn, my shoulder was on fire, and the magic backlash still raked at my insides, turning them to mush. All I wanted to do was fall into bed and sleep it off, but the night wasn't over yet, and those jackals would keep on coming.

I flicked my gaze up at the protection spellwork on the ceiling.

"Added some improvements," Shu said.

She had. I could see the new hieroglyphs and how they complemented those already in place. It was fine work, worthy of a display in a museum, but I'd expect nothing less from a demon sorceress.

"I also cleaned out your vodka and finished the Chinese takeout in the fridge."

That takeout had been a week old, but I'd seen her eat beating hearts. She could handle it.

"Did Bast drop by?"

"No. Just me, left behind, all alone." She jerked her chin at my arm. "Looks like you could have done with an extra pair of hands."

"We lived."

Chuck watched Shu with hooded eyes, the girl's young mind trying to wrap itself around what she was really seeing. Her skin was probably crawling off her bones.

"Are you two like...together?" she asked.

Shu barked a laugh. "You couldn't drown me in souls to touch his—"

"Bye, Shu," I butted in.

Shu snarled, and the temperature dropped a degree. She eyed me like she might argue. She'd grill me in the morning. Who was the girl, where had I been, what was really going on? It could all wait until the light of day.

Chuck continued to stand in the middle of the room after Shu had gone, eyeing my furniture like it might come alive and attack her. She'd seen some things back at the warehouse —impossible things. That had to make her take a fresh look at the people and things around her. She'd need time, weeks or months. Some people never adjusted to the truth.

"You can relax," I said. "This is probably the safest place in the city for you right now."

I eased Alysdair's custom sheath off, over my head and down my good arm. The sight of the sword tempted Chuck a few steps closer. With the blade sheathed, she couldn't see the glowing spellwork, but she couldn't have missed it back at the apartments. If she listened, she'd hear its low-frequency hum.

She reached out a pale hand. "What is it?"

"Enchanted sword. It eats souls." There was little point in beating around the bush when we'd already set the bush on fire.

A grin broke out across her lips. "That is so badass."

"Badass, yes, and also extremely dangerous. It doesn't discriminate. Good, bad, young, old—it'll eat everything."

"Where'd you get it?"

"My mother gave it to me."

Chuck worried her top lip between her teeth. "I never knew my mother."

I decided to leave that conversation well alone and busied myself with retrieving the first aid kit from the bathroom. Spreading the antiseptic wash and bandages across my desk, I pulled off my shirt and set to work cleaning my shoulder, keeping Chuck in the corner of my eye the whole time. She touched Alysdair but quickly pulled her hand back. She'd feel it, the slow pull, like the sword could suck the life right out of her bones.

She dropped her gaze to my coat and ran her fingers over the many ragged holes. "The sword and the long coat...some people who were kind to me back at the warehouse, they talked about a guy who scares off the undead. I thought they were nuts. Is that you?"

"Hard to tell. I've never met another guy with a sword who makes a living killing demons in New York, but hey, it's a big city."

"Is that what those dogs were? Undead demons?"

Where to start? I really wasn't in the mood for the big reveal, but when I looked at her face and saw her raw, needy expression, I couldn't keep the truth from her. She'd probably known she wasn't *normal* her entire life. If I didn't tell her, she'd go looking for answers and get killed.

"They're not undead," I said. "Demons are——" I pressed a dressing against my shoulder and hissed as the antiseptic burned its way into the bite. "The underworld, where they come from, it's brimming with souls. Some are lost, some like it there, and most are just passing through on their way to the Hall Of Judgment. But occasionally, a few stick around. They listen and they learn. They attach themselves to..." *Gods* just sounded too far out there, but what the hell? She was already looking at me like she might call the cops the second I turned my back. "Some devote their services to a few of the underworld gods. The influence of the gods, especially the darker demon gods, turns the souls into creatures like the jackals. Demons."

"That's how your sword was able to *eat* them?"

I nodded. "Then some idiot gets it into his head that ancient Egyptian spells look like fun, something to impress the girls with, and before you know it, you've got two demons possessing human bodies, contorting their DNA, turning them into creatures that shouldn't exist, and unleashing chaos in midtown. I tidy up the mess and try to avoid getting arrested, or shot, or bitten. I'm not always successful."

Her eyes couldn't get any wider. "Did that happen?"

"Yesterday—or the day before. I'm losing track."

"This is all real?"

"As real as the child you're carrying."

Her hand settled low over her stomach. "What does any of this have to do with me?"

"*That* is a very good question." I dug out a fresh shirt from my dresser and worked it on without igniting my shoulder all over again. With rest, I'd heal in a few days. Until then, I'd make sure to play the sick card with Shu—make her buy me some slippers.

Chuck ran her trembling fingers through her short hair. Chewing on her lip, she lifted her gaze to me. "I'm not normal, am I?"

"Not in the least." Leaning against the desk, I watched her process all the questions she had and whether she really wanted to ask them. "Being normal is all well and good until the demons are out to get you. You survived because you're not normal. You did well out there."

She looked again at my sword, its presence a constant reminder of how shit was as far from normal as it could get.

"Why don't you take a shower," I suggested. "Think over what you've seen and what I've told you. I don't have much in the way of food, but I'll whip something up. Once you're rested and fed, we'll talk some more."

I gave her some space to adjust, busying myself by microwaving two batches of flavored noodles. I tried Bast's cell a few more times, but each time it rang until her voicemail picked up. There was a chance she was deliberately ignoring my calls, especially after I'd brushed her off. Goddesses held grudges longer than empires reigned. But Bast would have set aside me acting like an asshole to know Chuck was safe. Something had happened to her between the modeling agency and the warehouse—something that was stopping her from getting in touch.

I returned to the lounge with two bowls of noodles. Alysdair thrummed, tempting me to pick her up and head back onto the street to hunt Bast down. But the goddess could look after herself. Chuck couldn't—not yet and not with demons on her tail.

I tucked the sword safely away in its slot wedged between the desk and the wall. When I turned back, Chuck emerged from the bathroom, hair knotted in a towel, wearing one of my shirts. She looked tiny, and pale, and vulnerable, and I had no idea what I was supposed to do with her.

I shoved the bowl of noodles under her nose. "Get that in you."

She dropped onto my bed and dug in.

I retreated to my desk and ignored the spreading, heavy tiredness. I needed to rest, needed to see Osiris, and needed to find Bast, but above all that, I needed to keep the girl safe. I hadn't expected to feel anything for her. Why would I? We were strangers. And yet there was something in me that had started to grow since Bast's return. I knew what it was. I'd experienced it before: *hope*. Hope that this girl might escape everything I'd been through and that maybe I really was capable of more than darkness. If I could save her, that meant something. Didn't it? I wasn't expecting that one good deed could wipe away five centuries of sins, but maybe it was a start.

After inhaling half her bowl of noodles, Chuck asked, "Why're you helping me?"

Because saving you is easier than saving myself. I hooked a shallow smile onto my lips, hoping it looked real enough. "Like I said, I get paid to help."

She accepted that and twirled her noodles on her fork. "Who's paying you?"

"Bast. The woman from the shelter."

More noodles went in. She chewed and then asked around a mouthful, "I've seen her in there a few times. She stands out."

"Yes, she does. Like a goth at a white wedding." I kicked back at my desk and worked on devouring my noodles.

"What's her deal?" Chuck dug into her bowl.

"She's one of the good ones." A little knot twisted tighter inside. Guilt and I were old friends. "There aren't many good gods."

Chuck's head whipped up. "She's a god?"

"Goddess Bastet—"

Her mouth fell open. "Goddess of Cats?" She saw my smile and said, "My foster mom taught middle-grade. She had a cool kid's book about Egyptian gods. The cat..." She blinked. "Oh. The big cat I saw...holy shit, that was her?!"

"That was her." I gave Chuck time to absorb that revelation and watched her look around the room as though seeing it for the first time. "She's also the goddess of pregnant women and the protector of those in need. Some women she takes under her paw, like you."

"This is insane." Chuck laughed, shook her head, and continued stabbing at her noodles. "I mean, shit. I... I knew she was different. Yah know, you can feel it. I can feel it.

Same as you...wait...what the hell are you, then? Are you an animal too? The eyes? You have—"

I waved her questions away, finished my mouthful, and said, "I'm not important. Don't even have a name. But you and your unborn child, you are important. Important enough to want dead." Setting the bowl aside, I brushed my hands together and leaned forward. "Chuck, I need you to answer me one question."

She wet her lips and blinked wide, innocent eyes.

"Who is the child's father?"

Her eyes clouded over. She looked into her bowl at the mass of noodles for answers and clearly didn't find any because her little shoulders shrugged. "This is gonna sound crazy—and stupid. I mean, I think I was high...but I..." She wiped her mouth with the sleeve of the borrowed shirt. "I don't know." A nervous smile darted across her lips. "Maybe I was high, or maybe I was roofied, but I'm careful. I look out for that shit. I don't remember anything. Maybe it was Immaculate Conception?" She laughed a nervous, tinkling laugh that held no humor.

There was another word for Immaculate Conception: Godstruck. She *had* been drugged, but not by any conventional means.

"You worked at the modeling agency?"

Her frown deepened. "Once, but they fired me when they found out where I live."

"Do you remember that one time you worked for them? Do you remember where you went and who you were with?"

She set her bowl down on the bedside table and pulled the towel from her hair, ruffling her tangled locks. "Sure, it was just some guy. He hired me to hang around with him and look pretty on his arm. It was just a few hours. I smiled and kept my mouth shut. I figured he was lonely or something. Pretty dumb, but some people pay for weird shit."

"Describe him."

"Tall. Nice looking, really. He had pretty eyes. Dark hair, tanned skin, like he came from somewhere exotic. " She frowned and scratched her head. "I dunno, just a guy. Nothing special."

I was certain magic had eaten away at her memories. She remembered only what the magic had deliberately left her with. "Do you remember anything else? What was he wearing? Did he have any assistants or mention any events?"

She shrugged. "Nothing." Her frown cut deeper. "Wait, there is something..."

My heart seized, already anticipating where this was going. "Go on."

"He drove one of those fancy electric cars. Not the ugly ones, but those sleek, fast-looking things."

"Color?"

"Black. Definitely black."

A black Tesla. Osiris. Fuck. All the fucks. Osiris was the father of Chuck's child, and he wanted my daughter and her unborn child dead. I'd suspected it, but the car, the car was key. Osiris. The one god nobody could touch. If he found Chuck with me, he would probably compel me to kill her, and I'd do it too. I slumped back in the chair and rubbed my forehead.

"You know who he is..." Chuck said, her voice small. "Was he someone important?"

I couldn't hide her in the underworld. He'd find her. There wasn't anywhere he wouldn't find her. Goddamn gods. He was tidying up his mess, probably before Isis found out he'd been screwing escorts and planting seeds.

"Ace?" Her small voice trembled.

"He's..." I wet my lips, met her frightened gaze, and tried again. "You don't remember anything because he's a god. If you spend any extended time in the presence of a god and they aren't reining in their magic, you'll end up godstruck. You won't remember anything afterward. It's how they get away with...everything."

She swallowed hard. "He raped me?"

Osiris wouldn't see it as rape. His perspective from up on his godly pedestal had been warped by millennia of worship. He'd probably consider it a gift that he'd chosen a lowly mortal like Chuck. "Yes."

A dangerous glimmer sparked in her eyes. "That fucker. I'll kill him."

"And I'd be right alongside you, except I've tried."

There was another way. I could bargain for her life. Trade something of worth. Osiris never could resist a good deal. Or I could trick him. Trick a god who'd lived seven millennia and seen it all? It'd be easier to bargain, but what did I have left to bargain with? He already had my soul.

"My baby is a god's baby?" Chuck pressed her hand to her belly. Her face had lost all the color she'd regained.

"It's a loose end, an unknown, and that's something all gods hate." I leaned forward, resting my chin on my steepled fingers. My gaze wandered to the protection spellwork above the bed. "There may be another way..."

CHAPTER 16

"Nameless One...kill the girl."

Osiris's mansion. Their bedchamber. The vast bed. I clawed at the memory—the dream—trying to tear it into pieces, but I couldn't stop it.

The blade cut through the young woman's throat like her skin was made of nothing but mist. I could hear myself screaming to stop, but the words never left my silent lips.

"I want to see you eat her soul." Isis's whispers poured into my ear. Her hand slid up my arm and over my shoulder until her fingertips fluttered across the back of my neck. My pulse raced so fast I could feel it beating on my tongue.

"Devour her soul." Osiris's compulsion tore through me, driving me to my knees. I caught the dying woman's face in my hands. Her brilliance shone, the light inside her welcoming and embracing me, like all good souls did. She looked at me, her eyes dulled by magic, and I fell into her as the two gods watched. The second I latched onto her soul, the consuming high gushed in. The deeper it flowed, the harder I pulled, so hungry for the light, until I had all of her embraced. And then, in that breathless, mindless moment, I wrapped the darkness around her and made her mine.

The liquid, intoxicating sound of Osiris's deep, rich laugh caressed my mind.

Isis's lips burned on mine. I thrust my tongue in, starved of her. She laughed and was gone, leaving me swaying on my knees, my soul burning, and the high riding me hard.

"Mm... our monster," the goddess mused.

The room shifted, or I did, and settled again. Osiris was gone, and the dead girl's body had vanished. Isis was lounging at the table, naked but for a gossamer gown. Blood clung to the edges of the crystal glass in her hand.

"Are you ever sated?" she asked.

I ran my gaze up her smooth legs, over her thighs and the curve of her waist, to where the wispy material clung to her breasts. I imagined my mouth there, my tongue running over her hard nipples. She'd arch under me, responding to my touch. Somewhere in the deep recesses of my mind a warning fluttered but soon died. Isis came alive under me—so smooth and so forbidden. I ran my hand lower. She parted her thighs, giving me permission. I kissed her lips, tasting honey and sweetness, and pushed my fingers between her legs as I drove my tongue in against hers. Breathless, I was mad for more.

A gasp—hers or mine—and I snapped open my eyes. My apartment, draped in shadows.

I darted my gaze around and straightened in the chair. The bed sheets outlined Chuck, asleep in my bed. Everything else was right where it should be. Nothing had changed. Nothing had happened. But my heart was racing, pounding its way out of my chest and pulsing hot blood through my veins. Adrenalin buzzed like an electrical current, as did magic too. Lust had me painfully aroused.

"Just a dream." I didn't like the way my voice trembled. Didn't like it at all.

Rubbing my hands over my face, I tried to sweep the dregs of the dream away, but they clung on like the whispers of the damned. Around and around the images spun, conjuring the taste and the feel of the goddess under me.

I staggered to the kitchen, flicked on the light, and blinked back into harsh reality. Coffee. Lots of coffee. Vodka too. Both would chase the dream from my head.

I searched the cupboards and found the empty vodka bottle. "Damn you, Shu."

A whisper of a warning tickled my neck and I spun around, lifting a hand to block—

Isis plunged a dagger into my gut and punched it right up to the hilt, delivering a shock of cold.

She caught my shoulder and pulled me into the blade, yanking me close. All I could see were the fine kohl lines outlining her brilliant eyes. Power pulled tight between us, mine and hers, but hers rose up like a mountain, filling the room, the apartment, the building, and folding in around me, making me small inside her embrace. She could crush me under the weight of it. The smallest of smiles in her eyes told me so. I was nothing to her, nothing but sand and dust.

She twisted the blade. Fire surged up my insides or ripped them out; I couldn't think around the pain to tell the difference. Her lips were on mine, her tongue sweeping in.

Withdrawing, she whispered, "Bad monster,"

I breathed her words down, feeling them harden like ice around my heart.

"The girl is mine."

"Don't..." I rasped.

"Mm," she purred, "aren't you sweet."

She pulled the blade out and stepped back. Weakness rushed in. If it weren't for the counter holding me up, I would have fallen.

"Nameless One...you should know by now not to interfere."

I held her gaze and felt her slippery soul moving inside her. "Let her go."

I couldn't help the compulsion; it came like a reflex, adding weight and intent to my words, but it washed right off her.

"Oh, that would be nice, wouldn't it?" She tapped the blade against her chin, leaving a smudge of blood—my blood —on her flawless skin. "But no. She's the last girl."

She turned and glided barefooted into the lounge.

I thrust out my left hand. *"San!" Stop!*

Isis laughed. The power in that laugh whirled around me, squeezing me tight, until it was all I could do to stay standing. On and on her laughter wove.

Chuck. I had to get to Chuck, whatever it took. Blood spilled between my fingers, slick and slippery. I fell forward, against the doorframe, smearing bloody handprints on the wall.

"Isis, please."

"Oh beg, please do. It's been so long." All around her the air glittered as if she were a being of light, of good. It was a trap, that light.

"Ace?" Chuck mumbled in a sleep-addled voice.

The ice around my heart shattered. Isis snapped her head around and fixed her sights on the girl sitting up in my bed.

"Run!"

I lunged forward, throwing everything I had into getting between Isis and my daughter. Isis merely swept her hand to the side, and invisible hooks punched through my chest, snapping me sideways. A moment of weightlessness took hold and then glass shattered around me. New York's din blared too loudly in my ears. A shock of cold hit me, and then my back slammed into the scaffolding guardrail. Without that, I'd have fallen fifteen floors.

"Ace!" Chuck yelled.

She didn't stand a chance.

"Wait. Isis. Stop." I dragged strength from somewhere inside and struggled to my feet. "Anything. I'll do anything. Don't hurt her."

Half stumbling, half falling, I scrambled back through the broken window and dropped to my feet. *Capable of more than darkness.* I could do this. I would do this—to save the girl.

"Ask anything of me."

Isis cocked her head. Her eternal eyes shone like jewels. "I did."

This wasn't about me turning her down. It couldn't be. "Something...there must be something. You wanna fuck? Fine, we'll do it now. Keep me for however long you want. I don't care." I held out my blood-covered hand. "Please. Just let her go."

Isis tapped the dagger against her thigh, leaving spots of red on her flowing gown. "Such a tempting offer, but really, this isn't about you. It's none of your concern, Nameless One. I kill the girl. All ends well. It's very simple. Look away if her death pains you so."

She took a step toward the bed, and Chuck scurried away, clutching the sheets against her like they might offer some protection. Her young, wide eyes swam with tears. She was brave, she was strong, but against Isis, that strength crumbled.

"Why? She's just a scared girl."

"The girl carries my husband's son," Isis snapped. "She must die."

"C'mon! This is Osiris. He fucks anything with a heartbeat."

"He is not supposed to impregnate them!"

"So the women had to die because Osiris lost his load?!"

Isis pointed the dagger tip at me and lined up her sights down the blade. "You do not stand in judgment over us!"

Yes, focus on me. Get mad at me. I stepped back, nudging up against my desk. City sounds buzzed behind me, and the cold air chilled me to the bone, or perhaps that was the blood loss hollowing the life out of my body. "Isis, you are the Queen of all Things. This girl is nothing."

"I don't *want* to kill her," the goddess waved a hand, shooing my argument away. "I have to. It is written."

"What is?"

"Thoth told me the son will sunder the king, my beloved. I do this for love, Nameless One. I wouldn't expect a monster like you to understand."

By the gods, a prophecy? Of course it was a prophecy. Nothing else would move Isis to act like this. "You don't need to believe the nonsense written by zealots. Thoth could be screwing with you—"

"Thoth doesn't lie."

That we were aware of. "My queen, you're more powerful than some thousand-year-old prophecy. The mutterings of mad priests are beneath you."

My heart pounded, squeezing my every breath. Blood was running through my fingers and down my waist, cool and wet —as cold as the chill spreading through my body. My life, draining away like the seconds I had left.

Isis's smile crawled across her lips. "Why take the risk?"

She moved in a blur of magic and mist.

I wrenched Alysdair free from its hiding place, raised the sword, and launched forward.

Isis sank her fingers into Chuck's hair, pulling her upright. Chuck screamed. Her wide eyes sought me out, pleading with me to keep her safe. I'd told her I would, but she would never be safe from the gods.

Isis pressed her blade against my daughter's pale throat. A bright droplet of blood welled. But I was there, Alysdair slicing through the air, so close. In a blink, it would be done. The sword sang. The blade flared, hungry for the god's neck and Isis's soul—

"Stop!" Osiris's command slammed into my body, yanking me up short. I dropped, but his wife didn't hesitate. She pulled the dagger across my daughter's throat, parting flesh, spilling blood.

The blade cut as cleanly as it had the last time I'd used it against another innocent's throat not so long ago. So quietly, it opened Chuck's throat, pouring forth streams of dark blood down her chest and silencing her scream.

I strained against Osiris's hold, the sword still buzzing, the power still lusting for Isis's death. Harder and harder I pushed, until my thoughts swam in the madness and my body turned to fire, but the compulsion held. With every second, every silent, reaching gasp, my daughter's chance of living her life died right before my eyes.

CHAPTER 17

Someone was screaming—a woman. The shriek sliced through the pain, piercing my soul. The power within broiled, and from it, a curse spilled from my lips. I'd curse them both and make them burn. With all the power of the underworld, with everything I controlled, I'd bury their souls.

"*Bae sra sudk, omd orr sros rok reqad. Bae sra kuir uk sruka I roqa cumkikad. Bae sra resrs, sra dord, Ikek, I cumdakm—*"

"*Seramca!*" *Silence*, Osiris boomed.

His glare pierced me as sharply as Isis's blade. The compulsion, and his power, thrust deep. I slumped over my knees. Silenced, perhaps until I died, which, given the amount of blood I'd lost, could be very soon. The terrible thudding sounded like a death knell and pounded throughout my body. With every beat, the numbness crept deeper into my bones.

"Husband!" Isis gushed. "It is done. You are safe."

Osiris's power shifted around him, flexing, pushing, and settling, but I wouldn't look. I couldn't.

"What is this?" he asked, mildly intrigued.

"She was the last girl. My gift to you, my beloved. Thoth warned me you'd been sowing seeds in fertile ground. From one such seed a boy would spring who would have ended your reign. Thoth never lies. I know you are busy with politics—with those stuffy men and their silly world—so I acted on your behalf. It is done."

I heard a sob and lifted my head. What was left of my heart broke as I watched Bast frantically trying to cover the gaping wound in our daughter's throat. It occurred to me, somewhere distantly, where my thoughts had gathered to be alone, that Bast had gone to Osiris. She'd told the god everything, hoping to stop him, but Osiris hadn't done this. We'd been wrong.

"Isis, my light..." Osiris crooned. "My love. Once again, you save me. Every day you save me."

"Wa roqa orvoaek baam susasrar. Wa verr orvoaek ba susasrar." she replied. *We have always been together. We will always be together.*

Bast roared. The sound shuddered through the floor and beat the air. Something wild, ageless, and primal had joined us in the room. She whirled on the couple, her fingers stretching into claws.

Isis flicked a hand. From the queen's fingertips a blast struck Bast mid-leap, tossing her against the wall.

Isis laughed. "Bad kitty."

I heard Osiris rain apologies down on Isis and the two gods declare their love like it was a glorious thing and not the twisted obsession that had killed a dozen innocent women. I might have fought, might have argued, but crippled with pain, chilled and suddenly so empty, I was done. I hit the floor, falling onto my side, and rolled my gaze toward the protection spellwork on the ceiling. I traced the design the way I always had. I *was* tired. It was time.

"As entertaining as your death would be, I'm not finished

with you." Osiris's warm hand settled on my abdomen. The other hand he placed over my eyes. Flesh spasmed, squeezing pain out of every cell. I'd have screamed if I'd still had my voice. He spoke old words, ancient words, words I didn't understand, and then, too quickly or not soon enough, he let go.

The god towered over me. His eyes narrowed and a displeased frown marred his timeless face. He looked at me as though puzzled, or perhaps surprised.

I blinked, and he was gone—Isis too. The combined weight of their presence bled away until all I could hear and feel was the cool wind, which brought with it New York's cacophony.

Bast's hands fluttered around my chest and came away glistening with blood. "Ace...oh, by Sekhmet. What were you thinking?" Her hands clasped my face, and she searched my eyes. A tear fell from her eye and tapped me on the cheek. "You stupid fool."

"Chuck..." I croaked. At least I had my voice back.

Bast shook her head and more tears fell. "I was too late. I'm sorry. I thought... I thought Osiris would stop if I could bargain with him. I didn't know it was Isis. *He* didn't know. I tracked her scent here, to you...she could have killed you."

I reached for Bast's face and brushed a thumb against her cheek, mixing my blood with her tears. "Chuck..."

Her hand caught mine. She clutched it close against her chest. "She's gone. I'm sorry, so sorry. I wish I'd never told you."

She buried her head in my shoulder, sobs racking her body.

Turning my head toward the bed, I fixed my sharpening gaze on the pair of gold-flecked eyes peering out at me from under the bed.

"Chuck..." I croaked. "Come out. It's safe."

Chuck slithered forward on her belly, crawling out from under the bed. She still wore my shirt, which was now covered in a few years' worth of dust. She coughed.

Bast lifted her head. She blinked at the girl, who was very much alive. Her face went from despair to rage in a split second, and the next thing I felt was a slap burning my cheek.

Bast scrabbled off me, onto her feet, and backed up. "What? How—I...?"

Chuck shrugged in that noncommittal way of hers. "Ace said it would work."

I'd admit that smiling probably made matters worse.

Bast's green eyes flared all cat like. "You bastard!"

She moved in for what would have been a decent kick had I not shifted sideways. Osiris's healing had chased away death, but I still had some healing to do. Healing that a kick to the gut wouldn't help.

"Hey! The dead girl was fake, but nearly dying wasn't!"

"I hate you!" Bast snarled, rumbling the walls again.

"I get that...a lot." Clearly nobody was going to help me up, so I hooked my fingers onto the bed and dragged myself onto my knees. The body was still there, in all its gory detail.

"I don't..." Bast mumbled. "I can't...she was dead. She's dead. She's there. How?"

I sat my ass on the bed and focused on breathing. That had been close—too close. I'd been ready and willing too. I'd have died to keep Chuck safe, a girl who deserved to live more than I did.

"Shukra switched my protection spellwork for an illusionary spell," I explained. "The body isn't real. None of it is real."

Bast marched to my bed and looked at me. "You brilliant bastard." She rounded the bed and touched the illusion of the dead body. "It feels real. I can smell the blood."

"It's a good spell." It had to be to fool Isis, although it had been designed to fool Osiris. "I can't dispel it while I'm drained. Would you do the honors?"

Bast hesitated, sweeping her eyes over the carnage, and then undid the spell with a few ancient words. The body and the blood shimmered and dissolved, leaving no trace. Above, the spellwork glowed and burned itself out.

Bast swore some more, throwing in some colorful, ancient curses for my benefit.

I looked at Chuck. She'd been hiding under the bed the whole time, listening to it all and seeing Isis toss me through a window. I'd told her to stay hidden—no matter what. It had been important that the gods sensed her inside the room. She'd hidden well.

She caught me watching her and smiled. "Is your life always this interesting?"

"Only on Tuesdays. What day is it?"

She laughed, and Bast cursed my name until she ran out of breath.

We'd survived the wrath of the gods, but it wouldn't last. Chuck had to run, far and fast, and she might never be able to stop. If either of them discovered she was alive, there wasn't anywhere she could hide.

I fell back on the bed and closed my eyes, exhausted, wrung out, and running on empty. "Wake me up for the next disaster."

CHAPTER 18

Chuck was wrapped up in a fur coat I'd stolen from Shu's office. Shu wouldn't miss it. She had hundreds. Color touched Chuck's cheeks where the cold wind bit, but her smile was warm.

She threw her arms around Bast, and they exchanged a few words. I hung back and settled for watching people file into waiting buses. They all had places to be, and Chuck would find hers.

Bast had given Chuck enough cash to get her started somewhere far, far away from New York. She was a good kid. She'd survived a brush with the gods. Few lived to tell those tales. I had faith she'd do just fine.

"Hey." She stood in front of me, her pale little hands stuffed in her coat pockets. "Thank you."

I smiled back. "Not necessary."

She pulled her hand from her pocket and held it out. I closed mine around hers, yanked her into my arms, and hugged her. Bast saw and looked away, but not before I caught her smiling.

"You're gonna do just fine," I said into Chuck's hair,

squeezing her a little too tightly, absorbing what I could of the moment before it passed. If everything went as planned, I'd never see her again. That was how it had to be, but it hurt in ways I couldn't describe and didn't want to think about.

"Sure I am." She pulled back and adjusted her backpack. "I wish I could stay. There's so much I want to know."

"Bast will follow once she's certain it's safe. There's a lot you *need* to know."

She hesitated, looked at Bast, and then back at me. "We're the same."

I'd been afraid she'd ask, but there wasn't a question there. She knew the answer. What I wanted to tell her, the things she needed to know about who and what she was—that was a conversation for another time and place.

"Try and control it. Don't let it control you." It was the best piece of advice I had, and advice I'd failed at.

She grinned and shot a finger-gun at me. "Stay awesome."

"Is there any other way?"

Bast and I watched her climb onto the bus and take a seat near the back. She wiped the condensation off her window and waved at us as the bus pulled out of the depot. Bast waved back while I did my best to smile as doubts poured in. She'd be fine, I knew that, but I would have liked to have time to get to know her and help her.

"She'll be all right," Bast said, sounding very much like the voice in my head.

"Yeah, she will."

"Are we doing the right thing?"

"Hell if I know." Judging by Bast's frown, that had been the wrong thing to say. "C'mon."

We started walking back toward the parking lot. Bast's gaze was as far away as my thoughts.

"If she'd stayed," I said, jogging down a few steps to where my bike was parked, "Isis would have found her. If her child is prophesied, she's a weapon, one any god will try to wield. It's better she stays away from us."

Bast sighed, but then she nodded and mustered up a smile. "I wonder if maybe I'd gone to Osiris earlier, he might have stopped Isis."

Stop Isis? I wasn't sure anyone could stop her, even Osiris. "Or he would have helped her."

"Have you heard from him?"

"No."

And that was playing on my mind. It had only been a day, but the god wouldn't forgive me for raising Alysdair against his wife and then attempting to lay a curse on them both. He'd make me pay for that. But I'd had to make the act look good enough to convince them the girl's death mattered, and to end it. Against the odds, it had worked. They didn't know she was alive, and they didn't know Chuck was my daughter. I planned to keep it that way indefinitely.

"I need you to do something for me." I leaned against my bike and fixed all of my attention on Bast.

She eyed me suspiciously.

Outside of Cujo and Shu, nobody knew what I was about to tell her. She'd hate that I'd lied, but lying was what I was good at. It wouldn't surprise her.

"Osiris did more than curse me to walk this realm and tie Shu to me. The curse...he can compel me to do anything he wants."

She tensed and tried to hide the shock from her face, but I saw the twitch in her lips as the snarl tried to break through.

"I have no resistance against him."

She blinked and her chest rose and fell quicker than before.

"Any word, any deed he orders me to do, I will."

"Since when?" Her two words were both sharp with anger.

I wanted to look away, to bow my head and fix my eyes on the floor, but I didn't. "It's always been that way. I don't like to broadcast it, for obvious reasons."

"There's a way out, surely?"

"No, I've looked. I can't get around it. Shu is the best sorceress there is and she can't unravel it. The things he's had me do... Bast, I..."

"You don't need to explain."

She held herself still as if she were tempering her rage. Her throat moved as she swallowed. She looked at me, and I wasn't sure I could stand to see the sadness softening her eyes. I didn't want her pity. It was why I'd never told her.

"I need you to wipe Chuck from my memories." There, I'd said it.

She frowned, and I knew she'd say no.

"If you won't, I'll get Shu to do it, but there's no knowing what she'll wipe from my head. I trust you to do it right."

"There must be another way?"

"There isn't. If Osiris asks me anything about that girl, I'll tell him. I've done worse. Much worse."

She closed her eyes. A muscle ticked in her cheek. "If I do this, you'll forget I was here."

"I know." *Was that so bad?* I wondered.

"I can't. I..." She pinched her bottom lip between her teeth. "It's wrong."

"And how wrong do you think it'll feel when Osiris learns Chuck is not only alive, but that she's our daughter and her *prophesied son* is still out there? You have to do this, for her. You've kept her safe for twenty years. This is just another part of that."

"You won't know you have a daughter..."

"I didn't know before, and it didn't kill me." But it hurt now, like a vise had hold of my heart and was slowly crushing it. To lose her again after only just finding her...it wasn't right, and it wasn't fair. I'd be alone again. But life was like that, and I couldn't say I didn't deserve it. "You have to do this."

"Yes." The sadness was back, pulling her lips down at the corners. "I'm sorry."

I tried to smile but didn't quite manage it. "We do it tonight. Before then, take me out to dinner at that fancy restaurant you took Chuck."

One last night. That vise around my heart squeezed tighter.

Her smile, small and fragile, was for my benefit. "I'd like that."

CHAPTER 19

I wore Osiris's borrowed suit. It was the only suit in a closet consisting of dark clothing only suitable for walking across rooftops at night. I'd considered shredding it and lighting it on fire, but Osiris wouldn't give a shit and I'd be down a perfectly good suit.

Bast had toned down her scary-goth look and wore a full-length, plum-colored gown. I'd told her she looked good enough to eat and then winced and tried to backpedal with disastrous results. She'd found my attempts hilarious.

We ate expensive food and talked about my business and Shu's early antics as a human-bound demon—anything but the gods. We even talked about what might have been, with Chuck, with a life away from the pantheon. It was fantasy, of course, but seeing as tomorrow I wouldn't recall any of the conversation, it couldn't hurt.

I should have known the gods wouldn't let me have one night of peace.

I didn't feel him approach. He had deliberately folded his power around him, tucking it in tight, allowing him to slip unnoticed through the real world until he'd eased into the empty space beside Bast.

"Do not move," Osiris said to me, freezing me in my seat.

Bast snatched up a table knife, but Osiris snagged her wrist and wrenched it, cracking bones. Bast let out a sharp cry and dropped the knife. And all I could do was sit and watch. Nobody around us batted an eyelid. Osiris must have cast a minor spell to shield us.

Osiris—the bastard—smiled, clearly delighted. "Isn't this pleasant."

"Why are you here?" Bast snarled, cradling her wrist. She'd be thinking of all the ways she could repay him for the broken bones.

"Don't," I warned her, already sounding as though I'd given up. Whatever was about to happen, the best thing we could do was play along and weather through it, and if Osiris was in a forgiving mood, it would end, eventually.

Osiris had kept his right hand hidden out of sight under the table, thinking he could hide what he'd brought along, but I could sense Alysdair's background hum. There was no good reason for him to go to the trouble of collecting Alysdair from my apartment and bring it here.

"You've had your fun, Osiris," Bast growled.

"No, what I had was a minor god tell me my wife was murdering women, and the Nameless One—of all the creatures—raise his sword against my beloved." His glare cut to me. "You attempted to kill Isis. That is treason."

"I..."

"Don't lie to me."

I shut my mouth.

"Isis has many colorful ways in which she'd like to punish you, but the task is mine."

I ground my teeth together. Clearly he'd brought the sword to use against me. There was a sort of ironic justice in that, which was typical of Osiris. He wouldn't kill me though. I wasn't that lucky.

He returned his attention to Bast. "Has he told you of his affliction?"

She glared at him but wisely stayed quiet.

"He has? Good. So you know the Nameless One is under my control. I wondered, at first"—he reached for Bast's half-finished glass of wine, leaned back, and took a sip—"what it might be like to have Ammit's student. Let's be honest, shall we? He's not known for following orders. He *was* the model godling...until his little addiction was discovered. So shocking it was that the underworld kicked him out." Osiris chuckled. "They don't shock easily in the underworld."

Oh yes, he liked the sound of his own laughter and voice.

"A stallion, this one. One made of scorching desert sand, like the *šarq*—a creature of myth that could not be caught or tempered. He was quite the presence in the Hall, a fierce beast to be sure, but one who could—and should—be controlled." He paused, probably sensing how I was straining against his mental shackles.

I tried to lift my hand off the tabletop, pushing every measure of strength I had into that one tiny goal. Just a twitch, that was all I wanted—something to tell me I could work around his compulsion. My hand didn't move.

"Make no mistake, Bastet. The Nameless One wasn't given a name for a reason. The most dangerous of our kind inhabit my domain, and to give one such as him a title would be...well, he'd likely unseat the Great Devourer—"

"Ammit is dead," I sneered. "Killed by the jackals as your *beloved wife* commanded."

Osiris blinked, and his smile tightened. "Ah, yes. Unfortunate. Still, slumber or death? It's all the same."

It wasn't, and to hear the god of rebirth speak so flippantly of life and death sickened me. "If you were ruling in the underworld, you could have stopped it, but instead you were here, playing the mayor, and your wife wielded your weapons. Isis makes a fool of you."

He worked his jaw and dropped his gaze. I fully expected him to silence me once again. When he looked up, he still wore the perfect act of an indifferent god, but his smile had lost its luster. "Do you have proof?"

"I witnessed the jackals tear Ammit apart."

"Did you see Isis command the jackals to kill your mother? The truth now. No lies."

I knew where this was going and growled, "No."

"Did anyone else besides you witness Ammit's death?"

"No."

His smile was back in true form. "The testament of the Nameless One, the infamous liar, is no testimony at all." Osiris sighed and placed the wine glass down on the table. "Her sudden demise certainly explains why you're wanted for your mother's murder."

My heart skipped a beat and my mouth went dry. "I didn't—"

"Where is her soul? In the great river, I presume?"

Fear lashed through me. I wasn't sure where Ammit's soul was. I hadn't stopped to properly weigh and judge all the souls I'd consumed in her chambers. Her soul could have found its way to the river, but there was an equal chance I'd devoured it.

Who was I kidding? I'd taken it along with every other living thing in her chamber. I'd taken it all.

Bast was looking at me with suspicion glittering in her eyes.

"I didn't kill Ammit," I said, pushing the words between my teeth.

"She gave you to me," Osiris countered. "A transaction

you've searched for a way to be free of for centuries. I'd consider that quite the motive."

My thoughts raced in circles. Anubis believed I'd killed my mother? The implications were huge. I had to speak with him, but would he listen? As Osiris had pointed out, I wasn't exactly the underworld's poster boy for obedience.

"It was Isis. She had control over your jackals. She sent them after Bast's women. Your wife did this, Osiris. You know it."

He didn't deny it. He probably knew exactly what had happened and maybe had even shared a glass of an innocent's blood while Isis regaled him with all the details. But like the bastard he was, he'd prefer to see me suffer than let his wife stand accused before Anubis.

"Why would she kill your mother?" Osiris asked.

"Probably because..." I bit off my sentence, finishing it in my head instead:... *your wife had her hand on my cock and I turned her down.*

Killing Ammit seemed extreme, even for Isis, but she was as screwed up as a bag of snakes and gods with damaged egos did crazy things, like stop the Nile from flooding, destroying a civilization in the process, or kill other gods and point the finger at me. If I told Osiris why, he'd probably stab me with Alysdair. I wanted to get through this conversation with all my body parts intact.

"Don't keep it to yourself, now," Osiris pushed.

"Ask your wife."

Bast's suspicion grew, shock and betrayal on her face. I wanted to tell her the truth, and I would, later. I had to withstand the guilt she was piling on. I chewed on my lip and glared at my hand, attempting to will it into motion. Just a tiny flicker —a little hope that his compulsion had weakened. Anything.

"I could compel you to answer."

"Yes, you could." I gave up and glowered at the god. "You won't like my reply."

Rubbing his fingers together, he considered it. Maybe he already suspected the answer.

"Was it your idea?" I asked. "To allow my safe passage home to see Ammit? Or did Isis whisper it in your ear?"

He didn't reply.

Isis had set me up.

"What's done is done," Bast said, the voice of reason. "Osiris, if we have offended you, I am truly sorry. Had Isis come to me, perhaps we could have stopped this bloodshed, but there is no use debating what might have been. What can I do to make this right?"

He turned his most charming smile on Bastet. "You, my dear Bastet, can do nothing. He, on the other hand, must pay a debt. Treason is a damning offense, is it not, Nameless One?"

Technically, no, but he didn't want to hear how a soul's weight was measured on good and bad deeds, not on whether the person happened to piss off the God of the Underworld. I'd consider that a damn good deed.

"Just get it over with," I growled.

Whatever degrading act he'd force me to do, I'd forget it anyway. Bast would take the memory away and I'd be blissfully unaware this conversation had ever happened or that the punishment had taken place—unless I was dead. But there wasn't any risk of that. He'd brought me back from death a day ago. Whatever he wanted from me, it wouldn't be fatal. I'd survive. Always had and always would. Like he'd said, he wasn't finished with me.

He heaved Alysdair onto the table, rattling the plates and toppling Bast's wine glass. The wine splashed far and dribbled off the edge of the table. I looked around to see if we'd caused a stir, but people continued chatting and eating their over-priced food.

"They can't see us," Osiris explained, and then added, "Pick up the sword."

My hand moved like it had a mind of its own. I had to stand to get a good grip, and my fingers curled around the handle. The familiar warmth spread over my hand and up my arm. I'd had the sword for so long that she was practically an extension of me—of my will—and an escape.

Osiris looked up at me from his relaxed position. "I want you to know, this was the lesser punishment."

Here it comes. I swallowed, sword in hand. "The bitch pulls your strings even now?"

Osiris's dark eyes flared gold. "Kill Bastet."

I knew I couldn't stop it. I knew, after centuries, that nothing could weaken Osiris's hold on me. I knew, as I thrust the sword through my ex-wife's chest, that it wasn't me doing this, but knowing didn't change the reality that those were my hands on the sword and it didn't change the feel of how the blade shuddered when it sank between her ribs, into her heart.

She gripped the blade, and I remembered how she'd reached across this same table not so long ago and told me I'd be okay. She'd told me I was capable of more than darkness. Even now, her eyes said sorry, like she knew what this would do to my soul. Something inside me broke and crumbled away. Alysdair sang, drinking down the lightest soul I'd ever known, and I hated the sword, hated what it could do, and hated that Bast had to suffer for all eternity because I'd screwed up.

I held her gaze as the light inside her faded and her eyes dulled. I wouldn't look away. Not this time. I owed her that much.

Osiris picked up my glass and drank down the wine.

"With that done, I have politics to juggle." He stood and flashed me a smile. "Enjoy the rest of your meal."

"*Daquir*," I whispered.

Ashes and ambers ate away at Bast's body until there was nothing left of her. I sat down and enjoyed what remained of my cold meal.

CHAPTER 20

S hukra found me sitting on my office floor, leaning back against the wall, surrounded by scattered papers and splintered remains of my desk and all its contents. I'd taken Alysdair to everything before thrusting the sword into the wall, where it had stubbornly stuck.

Magic whipped around me, dark and deadly. I didn't hide it. Didn't care.

It hurt, everywhere and nowhere. I wanted to tear out my heart and make the horrible, consuming emptiness go away or fill it with drink, or death, or something—anything. *Just make it stop.* I'd tried drowning the ache in vodka. Broken bits of the vodka bottle glistened on the floor around me.

Godkiller.

I pressed the back of my hand to my mouth, and curled my hand into a fist. Grief swelled inside like an incoming tide. I couldn't escape it. Through every barrier I erected, and every time I tried to sidestep it, the weight plowed inside, filling me up and hollowing me out all at once.

Shu was watching me, considering her words. I hadn't

looked up, but I knew she was there, careful to skirt the fringes of my power.

"What do you need?" she asked after minutes or hours.

It was a good question. I needed the curse gone. I needed to kill Osiris and make Isis watch. I needed to be better—to be someone who saved people and didn't kill them. I needed to be the man Bast had believed—had *hoped* I could be.

"I need you to wipe my memories."

Shu stalled again, treading on ice. "Which ones?"

Through the fog and the pain, I lifted my head and found Shu's face set in a grim mask. "Anything relating to Chuck and...and Bast. She didn't walk into my office. She didn't hire me. She was never here."

She blinked slowly and evaluated the destruction I'd wrought. "That will be difficult."

"Not for you," I drawled.

"Can I ask what happened?"

"No." I yanked off my wedding band, pulled my knees up to my chest, and rested my arms there. Light flowed over the ring, turning it to liquid gold in my hand. "Take this. Put it somewhere safe. Somewhere I won't find it. But..." My throat tried to close off the next words, so I cleared it. "But don't throw it away."

She didn't move. Her eyes darted to the sword sticking out of the wall and back to me, sitting on the floor. Her eyes, her stance, it all said no, but fear stopped her from denying me. It said a lot when the most proficient sorceress the underworld had ever produced was afraid of me.

With a reluctant sigh, she ventured closer. "I'm going to regret this."

I wouldn't. I couldn't regret what I didn't remember.

❦

THE SNOW WAS MELTING FAST, TRICKLING INTO GUTTERS and gurgling down the drains, as I pushed through the stained-glass door into the store Curiosities. The heat hit me first, like it always did when I stepped off New York's winter streets into Maf's store. Evocative smells of cinnamon and thyme tickled my memory. Old scents from an old world.

An electronic bell buzzed, its modern sound at odds with the rows of shelves stacked to the ceiling with artifacts, tourist junk, and witchcraft paraphernalia. Glass skulls sat next to dozens of papyri, their potency hidden among the trinkets.

The ancient and infallible Mafdet—Slayer of Serpents—was tucked behind the counter. Her ample bosom rested on the countertop, threatening to spill out of her flower-print top. She threaded a string of colorful beads through her fingers, drawing my eye to the valley between her generous assets. It had once been widely known that no god or beast could outrun her. Her fortunes had changed since then, but she'd adapted—adapt or slumber. There was no other way for the ancient ones.

"Back so soon, Ace?" she asked. Her voice was cracked with age, or so it would seem to those who believed she was the kind, but slightly unhinged old lady who ran a store full of superstitious nonsense. "Business or pleasure?"

"Business."

"Ah." She picked up a pair of wire-framed glasses and planted them on her nose. "You get more handsome every time I see you. Almost as dashing as the Lord of Silence."

My lips twitched. The Lord of Silence was yet another name for Osiris—Lord of Death didn't have the same poetic ring to it. "Flattery might work for Shukra, but not for me, Maf."

She *tsked*. "So serious for one so young."

I stopped at the counter. We weren't alone in the store—a

tourist couple was browsing the aisle—so I couldn't very well press Alysdair against Maf's neck and terrify the answers out of her, but that might change the moment those window shoppers left. Maf knew it too, hence the beads of sweat glistening on her brow.

"The kid I spoke to in here a few weeks ago, I warned him off, remember?"

She pursed her lips. "Something happen to him?"

"Now why would you ask that? Unless you sold him those canopic jars after I advised you to send them back to wherever you got them from."

"We all gotta eat." She winced at that and blinked quickly, remembering to whom she was talking. "It's not my fault the people with money are idiots. What did he do?"

"Summoned two demons."

She spluttered. "Not with those jars he didn't. They were inactive. Made sure of it myself. No magic in them."

"Are you sure about that?" I leaned against the counter. Her red-rimmed, watery blue eyes flicked to where Alysdair was peeking over my shoulder.

"I was assured."

"So you didn't check yourself?"

"Look at this place. It's full of hungry, needful little trinkets. They all chitter and tease. No, I didn't check myself. I just put them on the shelves, like everything in here." She puffed and huffed, apparently offended.

"Did you sell him anything else? Anything like a potent summoning spell?"

"N-no," she stammered. "No, I wouldn't. Never. Ace, we have an agreement. I help you, and you don't shut me down. I wouldn't risk that by touching anything with power. I wouldn't."

The browsing couple brushed by me, eyeing Alysdair.

"Cosplay," I muttered.

They smiled, chuckled nervously, and moved on to admire a simplistic painting of Isis's profile.

Maf wiped a hand across her forehead. Dark patches had spread under her arms and the fingers caressing her beads trembled. "I swear by Isis—"

"Swear by someone worth something."

She recoiled as though me bad-mouthing Isis would somehow cause my curse to rub off on her. I grinned back at her.

"I swear it. By Amun-Ra, I swear it."

Damn. I was hoping she'd sold the kid the papyrus spell so I could follow a paper trail to the source. My only lead had just gone cold.

"I believe you." Nobody swore on Amun-Ra's name and lied.

Her shoulders drooped, her relief almost tangible.

"But if anyone tries to sell you anything potent, I want to know about it—immediately. Not in a few days. You pick up your phone and you call me there and then."

She nodded frantically. "Of course."

"Good. Now tell me what this is?" I planted Ammit's box on the countertop and watched Maf's eyes widen and her plump lips form an *O.*

"May I?" she asked, reaching for it.

I gestured for her to go right ahead and watched her plant the box in her palm like it was made of glass.

"My, my. Such power."

I didn't reply and certainly didn't tell her I couldn't feel any power coming from that box. Someone had warded it against me personally, and that was information enough.

"Can you open it?"

She gave it a twist, but the lid didn't budge. "There may be a way, but it's sealed by expert hands. It will take time. Why don't you ask Shukra?"

"No, this is..." I wasn't sure why I didn't want Shu to know about the box. It seemed important that nobody know, and Maf was almost nobody. She could keep secrets. "This is private."

"I'll see what I can do."

"Tell me about Shukra's most recent visit."

Maf tucked the box away behind the counter and relayed Shu's visit to me, like she did every month. Shu didn't know Maf reported to me, and Shu also didn't know I was keeping a close eye on her magical practices. She thought she was slipping her on-the-side spells by me. So far, she'd sold a few spells here and there for a few hundred bucks. Love potions, prosperity spells, and the occasional minor curse—little things. But she'd get greedy. Greed was a sin we both shared in.

When Maf finished, she added, "She bought those ingredients in the last few days."

The ingredients, including a goat's heart, were potentially dangerous in Shu's hands, but a mundane household ornament could also be turned into a wicked charm in her hands. Still, I couldn't shake the feeling I was missing something, something vital. It would come to me.

"Looks like she's preparing a blocking spell," Maf supplied carefully, watching my reaction.

"Yes, it does." A blocking spell boxed up thoughts, dreams, and memories and tucked them far away inside the subject's mind. It was a difficult spell to master. I couldn't cast it, but Shu could. "Thank you, Maf."

When I reached the door, she called out, "Rumor has it there's a price on your head."

I'd heard the same rumor.

Godkiller, those same whispers said.

Anubis believed I'd killed Amy. He wouldn't come after

me himself, but he'd send others until someone or something caught me with my back turned.

"There always is, Maf." I shoved through the door into the shock of winter air and said again, to myself, "There always is."

SHU WAS PARTICIPATING IN A LOUD AND COLORFUL conversation on the phone in her office when I returned. Someone was getting an earful, and for once, it wasn't me. Whoever it was should be grateful. Shu's silence was far more dangerous.

I opened my office door and froze.

There, sitting on my desk like it had every right to park its rump on my day planner, was an all-black house cat. Not an alley cat. This one was well fed and groomed.

The tip of its tail twitched across its front paws.

"Shukra?" I called out, keeping my gaze leveled on the cat. "Shu!"

"What?" she snapped back.

"There's a cat on my desk."

"I didn't put it there."

"A *real* cat." The cat blinked its green eyes at me.

"What do you want me to do, call animal control? The NSA?" She slammed her door closed.

"I hate cats," I grumbled at the feline and stalked closer. It didn't have a collar, but someone somewhere was missing a pet. Its tail twitched again, and it looked back at me, daring me to shoo it off my desk. The second I did, it would probably turn into a spitting ball of claws and fangs.

"Cat, that's my desk."

It lifted a paw and started grating its pink tongue across its pad.

"Leave, cat, or I'll—" I reached for Alysdair. The cat's eyes flickered with knowledge, like the little feline was urging me to brandish the blade.

With a small laugh, I dropped my hand. "Fine. I'm going out. You better not be here when I get back."

But it was there when I got back, curled asleep in my chair. I would normally kick it out, but as I went to scoop up the creature, I hesitated. It wasn't so bad. Asleep, it was harmless.

"Yah know, the death sentence for killing cats was abolished long ago. I can make it so you meet your little four-legged friends in the afterlife sooner rather than later."

It didn't stir. Clearly this cat didn't have a shred of self-preservation.

I shoved the sleeping cat and chair aside and parked the guest chair behind my desk. The cat didn't wake, and now it owned my chair.

"I hope you like vodka," I told it while checking my planner.

Shu had stuck a note on today's date: *Mr. Cooper called. There's a talking alligator eating his thousand-dollar koi. Be there – 2:00 p.m.*

A job—exactly what I needed. "No rest for the wicked."

۞

CONTINUES...

THE SERIES CONTINUES IN **WITCHES' BANE, CLICK HERE to buy now!** or turn the page for an excerpt.

Don't miss new releases by signing up to Pippa's mailing list here: Pippa DaCosta's website. No spam, and you get free ebooks.

Did you enjoy **Hidden Blade?** Don't forget to leave a review at your favorite vendor. Just a few words will do.

☙❧

Turn *the* *page* *for* *a* *look* *at* *Book* *2*, *Witches' Bane...*

EXCERPT - SOUL EATER #2 - WITCHES' BANE

The Metropolitan Museum of Art had rolled out the red carpet for New York's mayor, otherwise known in exclusive circles as Osiris, God of the Underworld and God of Fertility, Rebirth, the Circle of Life, and everything in between. The museum's curators obviously didn't know he was a psychotic bastard—nobody here did. So charming, he'd singled-handedly reduced New York's crime rate by twenty percent and heroically helped birth babies in taxicabs. Ask anyone, and they'd say the sun shone out of his eternal ass. Now he was kind enough to loan the museum a priceless tablet from his extensive collection of Egyptian artifacts.

I would've preferred to slit my wrists than tag along with him, but after he'd been so kind as to invite me to this shindig, I couldn't refuse. Literally.

I stole a flute of champagne from a side table, wishing I had the hefty weight of my sword, Alysdair, in my hands instead, and lurked at the edges of the Seckler Wing. The *Temple of Dendur*—the original, shipped here from Egypt as a gift to the US from the Egyptian government—was backlit with dramatic, slowly undulating lights that cast a burnt-orange glow over the sandstones, the crowd, and the decorative pool—an artistic rendering of the river Nile. The entire exhibition was a theatrical delight that made Osiris smile from ear to ear.

I gulped down the contents of the glass, hoping it might settle my nagging restlessness and the need to palm my sword and devour the souls of everyone in this room. It didn't. Clearly, I'd need something stronger than champagne to get me through this.

I tugged at my suit jacket and pulled the shirt collar away from my neck. Where the expensive fabric chafed, my skin wanted to curl in on itself. It wasn't technically my suit. Osiris had lent it to me, apparently on a permanent basis.

Osiris hadn't bothered me in decades, but in the last three months, the god had kept me on speed dial for every charity function or political event he could think of. I was an odd choice for his plus one, considering I'd like nothing better than to watch him die a slow painful death. He knew it too. With a few thousand years of life tucked under his belt, Osiris had an acquired sense of humor.

My wanderings had carried me to the dais between the temple's "gate" and the main eight-meter-high temple building with its two impressive columns. A bone-deep thrum rippled beneath the chattering crowd. Magic. Even this far from home, through distance and time, the little temple clung to its power. It paled in comparison to its former glory. The resonance had once shone like a star but today it was nothing more than dying embers. Still, I felt its evocative touch wrap around me. Comfortable and warm. Familiar. Like meeting an old friend.

A waiter drifted by and I swapped my empty glass for a fresh one. Folding my free hand around the rail, I breathed in, momentarily forgetting everything "New York." In those few seconds, I could smell the sunbaked grasses, feel the warm spiced breeze on my face and taste it on my lips, and hear the voices of market-goers bartering for goods.

"Ironic, don't you think?"

Osiris's voice snapped me back into the present, where I was surrounded by fake smiles, too many people, and a suit that itched. A hollow sadness lingered. I hadn't thought of the homeland in months, and before that, not in decades. I was different now; the world was different. No use dwelling in the past. That road led all the way to insanity.

Osiris leaned against the railing, arms crossed and his face lifted toward the columns. In the sunset reds of the lighting, his dark skin took on the typical reddish, vermillion glow found in many of the statues that depicted him in all his godly finery. All that was missing were the crook and flail.

"They place our temples in temples of their own," he continued.

"It's a museum, not a temple," I grumbled. Petulance was my middle name.

His thin lips twitched, and he turned those dark eyes on me. Although he held his substantial power in check, his presence tugged on the glances of every man and woman here. Instincts warned them they were in the midst of something dangerous, but human instincts arced back to the days when they hunted on the plains with spears, and Osiris was exactly the kind of warrior they would've wanted by their side. Flash forward to the twenty-first century and everyone wanted a piece of him, but if asked, none could say why.

"They come," he said. "They yield their coin as offerings and walk among these relics, their whispers filled with awe."

There was little point in arguing with him. You can't win an argument with a god. And perhaps he was right. It was ironic.

"Dedicated to you and Isis," I said, nodding at the temple.

"Was it? I hadn't noticed."

Liar. He'd known. From where I stood, I could see his name carved in hieroglyphs in a dozen places. This temple, the museum, tickled his ego. That was what the secret smiling was about.

"Why give the museum the tablet?"

The tablet in question sat on its podium next to the various other exhibits against the far wall of the hall, away from the throngs of people. I'd seen it before in Osiris's private collection. The hieroglyphs had survived the trials of time mostly intact and depicted scenes of death and rebirth, Osiris's specialties. Tablets were often imbued with the magic of their owners, much like the temple resonating around us.

"Why not? I have dozens. It seemed like a nice gesture."

Nice. The way he'd said it, with a single eyebrow rising by little more than a millimeter and the corner of his lips curving in the same way, suggested there was nothing nice about the gesture. I'd never met a genuinely nice god. Bastet probably came closest, when she wasn't hunting down her targets and sinking her claws into their backs. *Nice* was a word that should never be uttered alongside the name of any god.

I had no idea what this god had planned for these people— it could be nothing—but I did know, without any doubt, that the mayor of New York was an eternal being with too much time on his hands. The gods hadn't stirred up trouble in thousands of years. It was overdue, like waiting for the San Andreas Fault to let go. When the gods did break, I didn't plan to be anywhere near the epicenter, which would be difficult if Osiris continued to drag me around like a dog on a leash.

"No Isis this evening?" I asked, wondering how much conversation was required before I could call it a night.

"No."

No explanation. No change in his expression.

I smiled into my champagne flute. Osiris I could handle—mostly. Isis was a whole other bag of snakes. Angry, poisonous snakes with fangs at both ends. Unlike her husband, she'd stayed out of my way, and I'd done everything I could to stay out of hers. Besides her occasional knowing glances, she hardly seemed to notice me. But I didn't like the knowledge behind those glances or how they peeled back another layer of me. I hadn't forgotten how she'd cornered me in her tropical garden, making it damn hard on me to resist her. How could I forget when my dreams were filled with what might have happened next?

Osiris had lifted his face to the temple again, and when a well-dressed middle-aged couple introduced themselves to him, I excused myself, downed the drink, left the glass on a side table, and started to filter back into the crowd.

Dislocated movement caught my eye. Beyond the pool, where the other exhibits were lit, four men moved separately from the crowd, their strides stiff with purpose. They were dressed like realtors out for a late-night drink after a busy day at the office.

I'd taken half a step toward them when the lights shut off, plunging the room into darkness. A few bleats from the crowd peppered the quiet. No panic, not yet.

Osiris's power rippled, casting an invisible and uncomfortable static surge across the room. My instincts kicked in, ready for an attack. Nobody here was crazy enough to go toe to toe with Osiris. Only a few gods would consider it, and most of them were slumbering the centuries away. But no such qualms existed when it came to attacking me.

A glass shattered against the floor to my left. Someone yelped. Panic nipped at the tension. Something was *wrong* here. A slow, sly, magical intrusion crept its way through the dark, but its source eluded me; it was like trying to identify one wrong note in a complicated melody.

Flashlight beams swept over the heads of the crowd and bounced off the dappled ceiling, scattering shadows in all directions.

"Everyone, please stay calm," an authoritative voice announced. "It's just a temporary glitch. We'll have the lights—"

The lights blinked back on, brighter than before, blasting away the party mood and illuminating a floor that *moved*. The crowd noticed the countless snakes writhing between their high heels and polished dress shoes and erupted into a screaming, heaving mass.

A few black-and-gold snakes slithered onto the dais. King cobras. And they weren't illusions. I dropped into a crouch, caught the gaze of one, and muttered the spellword "*San*"— Stop—while pushing a deep compulsion behind it to make sure the spell carried through every serpent. They stopped, frozen solid, alive and unharmed but now as dangerous as rubber toys. Snakes were easy enough to compel, which begged the question: why send them? A prank?

A smile teased at the corner of my mouth. Shukra would've loved the turn this party had taken. Osiris, on the other hand, did not. I straightened and wiped the smile off my face at the sight of him glowering down from the dais.

"Retrieve my tablet," Osiris hissed. A crack sparked up the wine glass in his hand.

My gaze shot to the tablet's empty podium, and right on cue, the alarms sounded.

Damnit. My freewill honed into a point of single-minded focus I couldn't control. I vaulted over a nearby railing, landed hard, and shoved through the panicked crowd into the hallway. The four men I'd spotted could have split up, but I was gambling on the fact they hadn't—and wouldn't. I'd seen that determined, glassy-eyed look before, in men compelled to act. I probably wore the same look, given that I didn't have a choice in my current actions. Osiris's order has hijacked my body. It was all I cared about, all I could hear, all I could see.

Retrieve my tablet.

I burst through the museum doors and out into the New York night. Traffic streamed along Fifth Avenue. Cabs were lined up at the foot of the many steps, but climbing into a silver Chevrolet sedan were my guys.

⚜

Ace's adventures continue in Witches' Bane - out now!

Shukra
SOUL EATER SERIES
www.pippadacosta.com

179

ALSO BY PIPPA DACOSTA

Soul Eater

Hidden Blade (#1)

Witches' Bane (#2)

See No Evil (#3)

Scorpion Trap #(4)

❦

The Veil

Wings of Hope - The Veil Series Prequel Novella

Beyond The Veil (#1)

Devil May Care (#2)

Darkest Before Dawn (#3)

Drowning In The Dark (#4)

Ties That Bind (#5)

Get your free e-copy of 'Wings Of Hope' by signing up to Pippa's mailing list, here.

❦

Chaos Rises

Chaos Rises (#1)

Chaos Unleashed (#2)

❦

Science-Fiction

Girl From Above #1: Betrayal

Girl From Above #2: Escape

Girl From Above #3: Trapped

Girl From Above #4: Trust

☙❦❧

New Adult Urban Fantasy

City Of Fae, London Fae #1

City of Shadows, London Fae #2

☙❦❧

ABOUT THE AUTHOR

Born in Tonbridge, Kent in 1979, Pippa's family moved to the South West of England where she grew up among the dramatic moorland and sweeping coastlands of Devon & Cornwall. With a family history brimming with intrigue, complete with Gypsy angst on one side and Jewish survivors on the other, she draws from a patchwork of ancestry and uses it as the inspiration for her writing. Happily married and the mother of two little girls, she resides on the Devon & Cornwall border.

Sign up to her mailing list at www.pippadacosta.com

www.pippadacosta.com
pippadacosta@btinternet.com

Made in the USA
Lexington, KY
14 July 2017